W9-ACV-998

A DOWRY *of* BLOOD

A DOWRY *of* BLOOD

S. T. GIBSON

Cover design by Duncan Spilling – LBBG
Cover photograph by Jeff Cottenden

Redhook Books/Orbit
Hachette Book Group
1290 Avenue of the Americas
New York, NY 10104
hachettebookgroup.com

First Hardcover Edition: October 2022
First Redhook Ebook Edition: March 2022
First Published in Great Britain in 2021 by Nyx Publishing

Redhook is an imprint of Orbit, a division of Hachette Book Group.
The Redhook name and logo are trademarks of Hachette Book Group, Inc.

Library of Congress Control Number: 2022934722

ISBNs: 9780316501071 (hardcover), 9780316521277 (Barnes & Noble Black Friday signed edition), 9780316501286 (ebook)

Printed in the United States of America

LSC-C

Printing 1, 2022

To those who escaped a love like death,
and to those still caught in its grasp:
you are the heroes of this story.

Author's note

This book winds through some dark places, and I want readers to be able to opt in or opt out at their leisure, so I've provided the following content guidance.

A Dowry of Blood contains depictions of:

- ~ emotional, verbal, and physical intimate partner abuse
- ~ gaslighting
- ~ war, famine, and plague
- ~ blood and gore
- ~ consensual sexual content
- ~ sadomasochism
- ~ self-harm
- ~ body horror
- ~ violence and murder
- ~ alcohol use
- ~ depression and mania

It also contains brief references to:

- ~ sexual assault (not directed at any named character)
- ~ drug use
- ~ drowning

A DOWRY *of* BLOOD

PART ONE

 never dreamed it would end like this, my lord: your blood splashing hot flecks onto my nightgown and pouring in rivulets onto our bedchamber floor. But creatures like us live a long time. There is no horror left in this world that can surprise me. Eventually, even your death becomes its own sort of inevitability.

know you loved us all, in your own way. Magdalena for her brilliance, Alexi for his loveliness. But I was your war bride, your faithful Constanta, and you loved me for my will to survive. You coaxed that tenacity out of me and broke it down in your hands, leaving me on your work table like a desiccated doll until you were ready to repair me.

You filled me with your loving guidance, stitched up my seams with thread in your favorite color, taught me how to walk and talk and smile in whatever way pleased you best. I was so happy to be your marionette, at first. So happy to be chosen.

~~What I am trying to say is~~

~~I am trying to tell you~~

ven loneliness, hollow and cold, becomes so familiar it starts to feel like a friend.

am trying to tell you why I did what I did. It is the only way I can think to survive and I hope, even now, that you would be proud of my determination to persist.

God. *Proud.* Am I sick to still think on you softly, even after all the blood and broken promises?

No matter. Nothing else will do. Nothing less than a full account of our life together, from the trembling start all the way to the brutal end. I fear I will go mad if I don't leave behind some kind of record. If I write it down, I won't be able to convince myself that none of it happened. I won't be able to tell myself that you didn't mean any of it, that it was all just some terrible dream.

You taught us to never feel guilty, to revel when the world demands mourning. So we, your brides, will toast to your memory and drink deep of your legacy, taking our strength from the love we shared with you. We will not bend to despair, not even as the future stretches out hungry and unknown before us. And I, for my part, will keep a record. Not for you, or for any audience, but to quiet my own mind.

I will render you as you really were, neither cast in pristine stained glass nor unholy fire. I will make you into nothing more than a man, tender and brutal in equal measure, and perhaps in doing so I will justify myself to you. To my own haunted conscience.

This is my last love letter to you, though some would call it a confession. I suppose both are a sort of gentle violence, putting down in ink what scorches the air when spoken aloud.

If you can still hear me wherever you are, my love, my tormentor, hear this:

It was never my intention to murder you.

Not in the beginning, anyway.

ou came to me when the killing was done, while my last breaths rattled through failing lungs. The drunken singing of the raiders wafted towards me on the breeze as I lay in the blood-streaked mud, too agonized to cry out for help. My throat was hoarse from smoke and screaming, and my body was a tender mass of bruises and shattered bones. I had never felt pain like that in my life, and never would again.

War is never valiant, only crude and hideous. Any left alive after the rest have been cut down do not last long exposed to the elements.

I was somebody's daughter once; a village girl with arms strong enough to help her father in the smithy and a mind quick enough to recall her mother's shopping list in the market. My days were measured by the light in the sky and the chores set before me, with weekly spoken mass in our tiny wooden church. It was a meager existence, but a happy one, full of my grandmother's ghost stories by the fire and the hopes that one day, I would run my own household.

I wonder if you would have wanted me if you found me like that: vibrant and loved and alive.

But you found me alone, my lord. Beaten down to a shadow of my former self and very near death. It was as though fate had laid me out for you, an irresistible banquet.

Of promise, you would say, of potential.

I say it was vulnerability.

I heard you before I saw you, the clink of mail and crunch of debris underfoot. My grandmother always said creatures like you made no sound when they descended onto battlefields to sup on the fallen. You were supposed to be a night terror made of smoke, not a man of flesh and blood who left footsteps in the dirt.

I flinched when you knelt at my side, my body using what little strength was left to jerk away. Your face was obscured by the dim night, but I bared my teeth all the same. I didn't know who you were. I just knew I would claw the eyes out of the next man who touched me, if my fingers didn't seize up and betray me. I had been beaten and left for dead, and yet it was not death that had come to claim me.

"Such spite and fury," you said, your voice a trickle of ice water down my spine. It rooted me to the spot, like a rabbit entranced by the hunter's lamp. "Good. When life fails you, spite will not."

You took my arm between your fingers, chill as marble, and brought it up to your mouth. Gently, you pressed a kiss to the pulse quickly going quiet in my wrist.

It was only then I saw your face, while you leaned over me and gauged how long I had left to live. Sharp, dark eyes, a Romanesque nose, and a severe mouth. There was no shadow of malnutrition or disease on your face, no childhood scar gone white with age. Just smooth, impassable perfection, so beautiful it hurt to look at.

"God," I rasped, coughing up bubbles of blood. Tears sprang to my eyes, half horror, half reverence. I hardly knew who I was talking to. "God, help me."

Drops of gray rain tumbled from the empty sky, splattering across my cheeks. I could barely feel them. I tightened my fingers into a fist, willing my heart to keep beating.

"So determined to live," you breathed, as though you were witnessing something holy, as though I was a miracle. "I should call you Constanta. My steadfast Constanta."

I shuddered as the rain began to pool around us, streaking through my hair and filling my gasping mouth. I know I had a name before that moment. It was a sturdy name, warm and wholesome like a loaf of dark bread fresh out of the oven. But the girl I had been disappeared the instant you pronounced me yours.

"You will not last long, steel-willed though you are," you said, drawing closer. Your presence over me blocked out the sky, until all I could see was the battered metal insignia pinning your cloak closed at your throat. I had never seen clothes as fine as yours, or ones that looked so old. "They have broken you. Badly."

I tried to speak again, but the pain searing through my

chest wouldn't allow it. A broken rib, perhaps, or several. It was getting harder to drag air into my body. I heard a sick curdling sound with every inhale.

Fluid in the lungs, probably. Blood.

"God," I rasped, managing a few meager words. "Save me. Please."

I squeezed my eyes shut and tears trickled out. You bent to kiss my eyelids, one after the other.

"I cannot save you, Constanta," you murmured. "But I can help."

"*Please.*"

What else could I have said? I didn't know what I was asking for, besides begging not to be left alone in the dirt to drown in my own blood. If I had refused you, would you have left me there? Or was I already marked for you, my cooperation merely a bit of formality?

You pulled aside my sopping hair and exposed the white flesh of my neck.

"This will hurt," you murmured, lips tracing the words on my throat.

I grasped blindly, heart hammering in my chest as the world blurred at the edges. My fingers curled around the first thing they found; your forearm. A startled look crossed your face and I clung to you tightly, pulling you closer. I didn't know what you were offering me; I just knew I was terrified that you were going to leave me.

You stared into my face, almost like you were seeing me for the first time.

"So strong," you said, tilting your head to take me in

the way a jeweler might a perfectly cut diamond. "Hold fast, Constanta. If you live through this, you will never know the sting of death again."

You lowered your mouth to my throat. I felt two pinpricks, then a searing pain that radiated down my neck and shoulder. I writhed in your grasp, but your hands were strong as a vise on my shoulders, pinning me to the ground.

I had no words for it then, the way we take our strength from the veins of the living. But I knew I was being subjected to some unspeakable horror, something not meant to be carried out in the unforgiving light of day. A fragment of one of my grandmother's stories flashed through my mind.

They feel no compassion, the moroi. Only hunger.

I never believed her tales of the dead who crawled out of the earth to sup the blood of the living. Not until then.

There wasn't enough air left in my body to scream. My only protestation was silent tears streaming down my cheeks, my body a rictus of rigid agony as you drank your fill of me.

Pain hot as the blacksmith's anvil burned through my veins down to the tips of my fingers and toes. You pushed me to the brink of death but refused to let me slip over the edge. Slowly, slowly bleeding me dry with the restraint only centuries taught.

Cold and limp and entirely spent, I was convinced my life was over. But then, just as my eyes slid shut, I felt the slick touch of wet skin against my mouth. My lips parted instinctively, and I coughed on the stinging, acrid taste of blood. It had no sweetness to me then, no depth or subtlety. All I tasted was red and wrong and burning.

"Drink," you urged, pressing your bleeding wrist to my mouth. "If you don't drink, you will die."

I pressed my lips tightly together, though your blood had already passed my lips. I should have been dead long ago, but somehow I was still alive, renewed vigor rushing through my veins.

"I cannot make you," you huffed, halfway between a plea and irritation. "The choice is yours."

Grudgingly, I parted my lips and took your blood into my mouth like mother's milk. If this was to be my only wretched salvation, so be it.

An indescribable fire bloomed in my chest, filling me with heat and light. It was a purifying kind of fire, like I was being scorched clean from the inside out. The ragged wound in my neck seared as though I had been bitten by something poisonous, but the agony of my bruised muscles and broken bones dulled and then, miraculously, disappeared.

Then the hunger started. Quietly at first, a stirring in the back of my mind, the gentle warmth of a watering mouth.

Suddenly it seized me, and there was no hope of denying it. I felt like I hadn't tasted a drop of water in weeks, like I couldn't even remember the taste of food. I needed the pulsing, salty nourishment streaming from your wrist, more and more of it.

I clamped my ice-cold fingers around your arm and dug my teeth into your skin, sucking the blood right out of your veins. I didn't have my hunting teeth then, but I gave it my best attempt, even as you wrenched your wrist away from my slick mouth.

"Easy, Constanta. You must remember to breathe. If you don't start slowly, you'll make yourself sick."

"Please," I rasped, but I hardly knew what I was asking for. My head was swimming, my heart was racing, and I had gone from nearly dead to viscerally alive in a matter of minutes. I did feel a little sick, to be honest, but I was also reeling with euphoria. I should be dead, but I wasn't. Terrible things had been done to me, and I had done a terrible thing too, but I was *alive*.

"Stand up, my dark miracle," you said, pulling yourself to your feet and holding your hand out to me. "Come and face the night."

I rose on shaky knees into a new life, one of delirium and breathtaking power. Blood, yours and mine, dried into brown flakes on my fingers and mouth.

You swept your hands over my cheeks, cupping my face and taking me in. The intensity of your attention was staggering. At the time, I would have called it proof of your love, burning and all-consuming. But I've grown to understand that you have in you more of the scientist obsessed than the lover possessed, and that your examinations lend themselves more towards a scrutiny of weakness, imperfection, any detail in need of your corrective care.

You tipped my face and pressed your thumb down against my tongue, peering into my mouth. An urge to bite swelled up within me, but I smothered it.

"You need to cut your teeth or they'll become ingrown," you announced. "And you need to eat, properly."

"I'm not hungry," I said, even though it was a lie. I just couldn't fathom having an appetite for food, for black bread and beef stew and a mug of beer, after everything that had happened to me that day. I felt like I would never need food again, despite the hunger gnawing at my stomach like a caged animal.

"You will learn, little Constanta," you said with a fond, patronizing smile. "I'm going to open whole worlds to you."

You kissed my forehead and smoothed my filthy hair away from my face.

"I will do you a twofold kindness," you said. "I will raise you out of the dirt and into queenship. And, I will give you your vengeance."

"Vengeance?" I whispered, the word harsh and electrifying on my tongue. It sounded biblical, apocalyptic, beyond the grasp of human experience. But I wasn't human anymore, and you hadn't been for a long time.

"Listen," you said.

I fell silent, ears perking up with newfound sharpness. There was the clanking of armor and the low chatter of men, far enough away that I would never have been able to hear it before, but not so far that we couldn't close the distance between us and them in a matter of minutes.

Liquid rage pooled in my stomach and lit up my face. It made me strong, that rage, hardened to solid iron in my limbs. All of a sudden, I wanted to destroy every man who had beat my father until he stopped moving, held torches to our home while my brother screamed for them to spare the children inside. I wanted to break them, even more slowly and painfully than they had broken me, leave them bleeding out and begging for mercy.

I had never been inclined to violence before. But then again, I had never borne witness to acts so vile they demanded retribution. I had never experienced the kind of agony that leaves the mind coiled and poised to lash out at the first opportunity. I would carry that viper inside me for years, letting it out intermittently to rip the wicked to pieces. But that day, I had not yet befriended the serpent within. It seemed to me a strange interloper, a frightening thing, demanding to be fed.

You put your mouth close to my ear as I stared off into the distance towards where the raiders were enjoying their meal. Even now, I have no idea how they stomached taking their supper feet away from the disemboweled entrails of women and children. War is the whetstone that grinds down all sense, all humanity.

"They will not hear you coming," you murmured. "I will stand a little way off to ensure your safety, and to make sure none of them run."

My mouth watered, aching gums screaming out. My stomach twisted into painful knots, as though I hadn't eaten in a fortnight.

Slowly, the shaking hands at my sides curled into steady fists.

I felt you smile against my skin, your voice taking on the rough pleasure of the hunt.

"Water your mother's flowers with their blood."

I nodded, my breath coming shallow and hot.

"Yes, my lord."

y lord. My liege. Beloved. King. My darling. My defender.

I had so many names for you in those days, my cup of devotion overflowing with titles worthy of your station. I used your name, too, the one your mother had given you, but only in our most intimate moments, when I comforted you during your rare displays of weakness or made a vow to you as a woman, as a wife.

But I am not your wife anymore, my lord, and I don't think you ever truly saw me as a whole woman. I was always a student. A project. An accessory in the legal and decorative sense.

You did not let me keep my name, so I will strip you of yours. In this world, you are what I say you are, and I say you are a ghost, a long night's fever dream that I have finally woken up from. I say you are the smoke-wisp memory of a flame, thawing ice suffering under an early spring sun, a chalk ledger of debts being wiped clean.

I say you do not have a name.

loodlust brings on a delirium that's difficult to describe. From the first squirt on the tongue to the last dying jerk of your prey under your hands, the whole experience builds and builds into a screaming fever pitch. Those with little imagination have compared it to carnal climax, but I liken it more to religious ecstasy. I have never felt more truly alive in my waking death than when I am taking the life of another person.

I didn't start small, with the gentle siphoning of blood from a lover in bed. I launched myself into the midst of my attackers like a fury from myth.

And I didn't just kill them. I tore them to pieces.

There were five or six men. I hadn't been able to keep count when they attacked, and I didn't bother counting them when I descended. They seemed to be one writhing, pulsating mass, a horde of insects best eradicated in a furious stomp of my boot. Before you found me, I wouldn't have been able to fight off one of them, let alone half a dozen. But your blood made me strong, stronger than any human had a right to be. It evaporated my fear and propelled me forward into their ranks, my mouth twisted into a snarl.

One of them looked over his shoulder and saw me coming, his face half-illuminated by the cooking fire.

He opened his mouth to shout. I wrapped my fingers around his upper and lower sets of teeth and wrenched his jaw apart before he had the chance.

The others fell so easily. I gouged eyes, snapped necks, fractured ribs, tore open the tender flesh of inner arms with my burgeoning teeth. My gums split, mingling my blood with the blood of my assailants, as I fed from them again and again. Only one of them tried to flee, staggering into the dark and right into your arms. You broke his leg with a swift, efficient kick, then sent him hobbling back my way like a parent turning around a wind-up soldier wandering too close to the playroom door.

When it was over, I stood unsteadily amidst the bodies, panting hard. I was satisfied with what I had done, with no treacherous regret creeping in at the edges, but I didn't feel exactly . . . satiated. The hunger was still there, quiet but present despite my churning stomach full of blood, and I didn't feel as clean and vindicated as I had hoped. The horror of being beaten while my family burned to death still existed, seared into my memory though my body no longer bore the marks. The appetite for revenge those men had sown in me was still there, curled up tight and sleeping fitfully.

I gasped for air, a sob bubbling up inside me. I didn't

know why I was crying, but tears bore down on me like an oncoming storm.

"Come," you said, draping me in your cloak.

"Where are we going?" I asked, already staggering after you. The bodies lying in a desiccated heap around the still-smoldering fire were hideous, but not half as gruesome as what had been done to my entire village, my family.

You shot me a thin smile that made my heart swell.

"Home."

Your home was half in ruins, covered by the slow creep of ivy and time. It was perched high above the village, in the craggy mountains where few of the common people ever ventured. Crumbling and faded, it looked almost abandoned. But all I saw was splendor. The fine parapets and oak doors and black peering windows. The way the tips of the towers seemed to puncture the gray sky, calling forth thunder and rain.

I began to tremble, looking at that fine house towering over me like it meant to devour me. By that point, the drunkenness of blood and vengeance had worn off. Fear stirred in my stomach.

"All within it is yours to command," you said, leaning down. You were so tall, and had to bend towards me like a tree in the wind to whisper in my ear.

In that moment, my life was not my own any longer. I felt it slipping away from me the way girlhoods must slip from women who are given proper church marriages and cups of communion wine, not bruising kisses and battlefields full of blood.

"I . . ."

My voice wavered and so did my knees. You must have sensed my weakness. You always did.

You scooped me up into your arms as though I weighed no more than a child, and carried me across the threshold. You held me so gently, careful not to grip too hard or leave any bruises. I was more shocked by your tenderness than by your miraculous arrival at the moment of my death. In hindsight, I should have paid more attention to the convenience with which you arrived. There are no angels in this world to accompany the dying in their final moments, only pickpockets and carrion birds.

I want to believe you weren't just playing your part. I want to believe your kindness was not just another note in the well-rehearsed aria of your seduction, trotted out countless times for countless brides. But I have loved you too long to imagine you do anything without an ulterior motive.

The foyer gaped open in front of me like a hungry maw. Cool shadows fell around us as we crossed the threshold, and the tarnished finery of the home took my breath away. Every detail, from the iron candle sconces on the wall to the brightly colored rugs underfoot, boggled my mind. I had known a very simple existence before then, happy but unadorned. The only gold I had ever seen was the gleaming chalice the priest produced from his sack when he traveled from a nearby larger city to administer communion twice a year. But now it glinted out at me from nooks and shelves, giving the whole room an air of sacredness.

"It's beautiful," I breathed, tipping my face to follow the line of the rafters until they disappeared into vaulting darkness.

"It's yours," you said. No hesitation. Was this the moment we were joined in marriage, when you offered me a share in your crumbling kingdom? Or was it when your blood first spurted into my mouth?

You kissed me coldly and chastely, and then set me down on the floor. Our footsteps reverberated through the home as you led me towards the stone staircase. You were sure to retrieve a flaming torch from the wall before leading me deeper into the shadows. Already, my ability to see in the dark was better than ever, but I was not as strong as you yet. I still needed the assistance of a little light.

Rooms passed in a blur of gray stone and tapestries. I would come to know them all, in time, but that night I could scarcely tell them apart. The house seemed bottomless, endless. I had never set foot in a building so large, and we seemed to be the only living creatures inside it.

Well. If you can truly call things like us living.

"Are you alone here?" I asked quietly. My filthy feet were leaving a trail of blood and mud on the carpet, and I wondered who would clean it up. "Where are the servants?"

"Fled or dead," you said, and offered no further explanation. "We ought to get you cleaned up, shouldn't we?"

You led me into a small room, and methodically began lighting candles. There was a long, shallow brass tub in the middle of the room, with buckets for ferrying water beside it. Tiny bottles of oil and perfume were scattered about on the rug, the kind of bottles one might find in a queen's bedroom.

"This is for me?" I said quietly. My voice was shaking. My feet stung from the long walk and every muscle in my body sang with the pain of dying slowly into a new life. With my bloodlust spent, I was unsteady on my legs. The whole night started to feel like a blurred, ecstatic dream.

"Of course," you murmured. "You deserve every bit of it. I'll draw your water."

I sat stunned as you filled the bath with steaming buckets of water, alternating boiling and cool until the bath was the perfect temperature. Then you pulled me to my feet and began to deftly unlace my outer dress.

I jolted away with a strangled sound. I had been willing and limp as a doll in your hands up until that point, accepting every touch, every kiss. But fear rose in my throat.

"Don't," I cried. "I don't want . . . I've never been looked at before. Like that."

Your brow furrowed in concern, or perhaps baffled irritation, but either way you lifted your hands gently from my clothes.

"I will never lift a hand against you, Constanta," you said quietly. "Never in anger, or in lust."

I nodded, swallowing hard.

"Thank you. And thank you for handing those monsters over to me."

"I would deliver a dozen men a day to feed your appetite if you asked me. I would round up every man, woman, or child who ever said a harsh word to you and trot them out for you on their hands and knees on a short leash."

"Thank you," I said, quiet as a prayer.

"Do you want me to leave you?"

"No," I said, clutching your arm. "Stay. Please. Just. Give me a moment."

You nodded and bowed shortly at the waist, then politely turned your back as I unlaced my dress and stepped out of it. My clothes were heavy with misery and dried blood, and I kicked them into a corner as they fell off my body piece by piece. I never wanted to see them again.

Then I stepped one trembling bare foot into the tub, sinking into the warm, delicious embrace. Within moments the clear water had turned blush-pink and then hawthorn berry red, obscuring my nakedness below. The water stung my open wounds, but they were already healing faster than they had any right to.

"You can look now," I said.

You knelt by my side on the ground, bringing one of my wrists up to your lips.

"Still beautiful," you said.

You bathed me as though I was your own daughter, rinsing the blood from my hair. I soaked in the tincture, perfumed by the agony of my abusers, and let you comb out every snarl.

"Tip your head back."

I did as you ordered, letting the water run through my hair. I always did as you ordered, in those days.

I had never even seen a bathtub any finer than a rough-hewn wooden trough before. The gleaming brass was cool against my skin as I shut my eyes and drifted, lost to the gentle touch of your hands and the dull throb of pain leaving my body. I felt as though I was floating above myself, watching you trail those long nails through my hair. It was tempting to slip away entirely.

"Come back to me, Constanta," you said, turning my chin towards you. "Stay here."

You kissed my mouth with an insistence that was already becoming familiar to me, until I melted under your touch and parted my lips for you. Water streamed from my body in rivulets as I enfolded you in my arms, suddenly emboldened. You ran your hands over my slick skin and made a sound like a man agonized. I knew then I would chase your tiny moments of weakness all the way into hell and back. What is more lovely, after all, than a monster undone with wanting?

"Let's get you dry before you catch cold," you murmured, still chasing my kiss. Your lips traced the curve of my chin, the slope of my throat.

I sat awkwardly in the bath as you retrieved a heavy housecoat and held it up for me, turning your face away behind the cloth. I stood and let you wrap me up, squeeze the water from my hair inch by precious inch. We left the bloodied dress on a heap on the floor. I would never see it again, after that night. I often wondered if you burned it, along with the final vestiges of the name my parents gave me. Either way, you enfolded me in your arms, pressing me to your body like I might disappear if you didn't hold me tight enough.

"Take me to your room," I said, clutching your clothes. It was an improper thing to ask, but you had already dissolved so many of the taboos of my previous life in one fell swoop. What indiscretions were left, after the sins we had committed together?

"I've prepared your own rooms for you," you said mildly. Ever gallant, ever pacing the stage of your own design, saying your right words.

Tears trickled down my cheeks at the thought of an instant of night without you close at my side. Quietness seemed to me a creeping sickness, one that would infect my brain with images of the horrors of that night. I didn't want to see my father's charred face again, to remember the screaming of the raiders. I just wanted peace.

"I don't want to be alone. Please."

You nodded, sweeping open the door for me.

"Whatever my wife wishes is granted to her. Let there be no secrets between us, Constanta. No divisions."

I cannot remember the details of your room that first night, only the gentle contours of complete darkness, of heavy damask and carved wood beckoning me in deeper. At the time I thought it felt like a womb, nurturing and soft-edged. Now I only remember it as the tomb where we slept through our living death.

You produced a nightdress of fine, soft linen for me

and welcomed me into your bed. I pressed my body against yours, the house totally silent except the sound of my breathing and the slow, steady pulse of your heartbeat. Too slow, like your body was only playing at a process it had long ago stopped needing. I couldn't get close enough to you to make the numbness creeping over my skin go away. I needed to be touched, to be held in a way that made me feel real. I feared I would slip away into horrible memories of my family being burned alive. Or even more frightening, into sheer, blank nothingness.

"Kiss me," I said suddenly, my voice ripping a hole in the silence.

"Constanta," you murmured indulgently, turning your face towards mine. Your lips traced a light line over my cheekbones, my chin. "Constanta, Constanta."

It almost put me in a trance, to hear you call me that. My skin burned unnaturally hot as I kissed you, over and over again until I was shaking. I don't know if I trembled for fear or want, or because my body was still breaking itself into pieces and being remade. The change takes days, weeks even, to take full effect. We mature over hundreds of years, moving every night a little further away from our humanity.

I was young, then. I would have let you do anything to make the burning stop.

"Take me," I whispered, my tingling lips brushing against your own. "I want you to."

"You're still weak," you warned, your hand already sliding up my thigh to rest on my hip. Your mouth moved lower, pressing bruising kisses into the crook of my neck. "You need sleep."

"I need you," I said, tears springing to my eyes. I wanted to scrape out some little joy from the harsh, ugly world, to find sweetness despite all the blood and screaming. I wanted this, I reminded myself. It was all that would make me feel strong and whole again. "Put out the light."

You did as I asked, plunging the room into total darkness, and then your mouth was on mine with a ferocity that almost frightened me. I sensed pure, exquisite violence behind your kiss, a desire to rend and devour that reminded me more of a wolf than a man. Your hunger for me was always more apparent under the cover of darkness, when you didn't have to arrange your face into any semblance of civility. I was always your little mouse, kept in a gilded cage until it was time for the cat to play. You never hurt me, but you delighted in my racing heartbeat, my frightened gasps.

Your fingers found the hem of my dress and deftly lifted it over my head. I trembled, pressed skin to skin to you as you moved your mouth over my collarbones and breasts with increasing insistence. You were not my first, but this was something entirely different than a giggling, fumbling encounter behind a barn with my childhood sweetheart. This felt cosmic, like a piece of me was being excised so it could take up residence in you.

"Open your mouth," you said.

You nipped your index finger with the sharp edge of

your tooth, then circled it around my lips to coax my obedience.

Blood smeared my lips in a slippery kiss until I opened my mouth for you. I let you slide your fingers inside and I circled them with my tongue, sucking you clean.

"No teeth," you ordered, and pressed your heat into the deepest part of me.

Do you remember how I trembled, valiantly battling with my new instincts? My mouth watered and my gums ached, but I obeyed you. Was it a test? Like holding a piece of meat in front of a dog and commanding it to sit, just to push the limits of its obedience?

I drank from you drop by agonizing drop as you slid all the way inside me, obliterating any memory of a life before you.

I slept for days after that first night, waking only to sup on thimbles of your blood. I tossed and turned, desperate for water, for my mother, for the long dream of my life to be over. The change was agonizing and slow, a calcifying of entrails and re-ordering of muscles. My skin turned from delicate flesh to smooth, unmarked stone, and my hair and nails grew a quarter-inch every day. Only my heart remained the same, faithfully pumping hot blood through veins that burned with my every tiny movement.

You tended to me with the faithfulness of a nun attending the dying, daubing my forehead with a cool washcloth, washing me and dressing me, and trimming my hair every night by candlelight. I eventually adjusted to our sleep schedule, waking in the evening and falling back into a tormented slumber as soon as the sun threatened to rise. And you were always there, steadfast and wise, shushing me wordlessly as you kissed me.

When I was well enough, we made love, my fingers digging into your flesh with the mating drive of a creature who knew it was dying. When I wasn't, you read to me or plaited my hair. I didn't know where you went when you weren't with me, but you were almost always there.

My savior. My teacher. My guiding light in the dark.

I think, my lord, that this is when you loved me best. When I was freshly made, and still as malleable as wet clay in your hands.

wish I had a better sense of time, or any sense at all. I wish I could insert dates and chart the rise and fall of our lifetimes exactly. But I was caught in the slipstream, washed out into the vast sea of you. You were the air I breathed and the blood in my nursing cup; I knew nothing else except the strength of your arms and the scent of your hair and the lines of your long white fingers. I lost myself so entirely in charting the contours of my love for you that there wasn't any room for tracking time. There wasn't any room to examine the past or the future; there was only the eternal now.

Eventually, I emerged. Whole and new, and somebody else entirely. The village girl I had been was well and truly dead. She had died a dozen little deaths in that marriage bed, and I was your Constanta, your dark and unbreakable jewel.

Eventually, you permitted me to wander the halls of my new home. Leaving the house was strictly forbidden, (I was still too weak, you said) and you fed me solely from your own veins in those early days. Occasionally you tempted home a boy from a neighboring village with the promise of work, but those feasts were few and far between. You did your best to only hunt for yourself when I was asleep, not wanting to leave me alone for long periods of time, but whenever I woke to an empty house I entertained myself with exploration.

I was so enamored with every painting, every carefully laid stone in the fireplace hearth. It was finery beyond my wild imaginings, and it was all mine to possess and command. Not that there was much to command, without any servants or guests or other living creatures in the house besides you and I. But I took great pleasure in rearranging furniture, dusting off family silver, and imagining what it might be like to throw a grand dinner party in the house someday.

No room was off-limits to me except the banquet hall, which I was to enter only with your express permission and accompaniment. One day, when you were feeling particularly magnanimous and I was giving you my sweetest pleading look, you granted me entry.

"This is a sanctum," you said sternly at the door. "Being permitted entry is a privilege. Do not touch anything, Constanta."

I nodded wordlessly, practically vibrating with excitement.

It must have been used for entertaining traveling gentry with lavish meals once. But you had cleared away the high-backed chairs and most of the tables to make room for all your beloved devices.

I didn't know what to call any of them then, but now I know I was looking at beakers and abacuses, mechanical compasses and astrolabes. All manner of medical and scientific tools both rudimentary and advanced, from Greece, Italy, Persia, and the vast reaches of the Caliphate's empire beyond. They were laid out in gleaming heaps atop sheaves of parchment. Some of the devices were well-used and others appeared to not have been touched in a century.

"What is all this?" I breathed, my voice carrying easily in the cavernous space. Everything about that castle made my tiniest word seem huge, disruptive to the ecosystem you had built.

"The best this backwater has to offer," you said, sweeping aside a chart of the constellations. "Such a coarse time we live in, Constanta. The greatest minds of Europe cannot riddle out the simplest diseases or equations. In Persia, they chart the course of blood through the body, operate on the livers of live men, perform feats of engineering that seem like alchemy to the untrained eye. The Greeks and Romans knew sciences that have been utterly lost to time."

"But what is it all for?"

"To uncover the mysteries of the body, of course. To catalogue the human animal and uncover its intricacies."

"I didn't realize you had such an interest in humans," I murmured, reminding myself that I could no longer count myself among their number. Human beings were a less evolved creature, you said, wretched short-lived beasts suitable for food and diversion and little else. Certainly not true companionship. I should not attempt to forge any friendships outside our home, you warned me. They would only end in heartbreak.

"I have an interest in my own condition and so I must have an interest in theirs," you said, running your finger over a page covered in tight handwriting. I couldn't read in those days, but I could recognize drawings of human feet and hands, a rudimentary sketch of what looked like a heart. "Don't you wonder what power animates us after our first death? Grants us our long, unaging lives?"

I gave a little shiver in the drafty hall. I tried very hard not to think about that, most days.

"I couldn't imagine, my lord. There is no creator other than God, so maybe He forged the first vampire from the clay of the Earth. Instead of mixing the clay with water, He mixed it with blood."

I had always been a faithful person, sometimes bordering on superstitious. Entering my second life hadn't changed that; it had simply broadened my existential horizons.

You smiled at me. Condescendingly. Almost pityingly.

"Your priest's bedtime stories cannot account for us. Whether we are nature's triumph or her great shame, there's rhyme and reason to our hungers. To our bodies and their processes. It is my intention to unravel it, to comprehend and map our condition."

"To what end?" I asked. I could not stop the questions from coming, even though I was learning that more than two in a row tended to irritate you. Sure enough, I saw a flash of annoyance in your eyes. But you sighed and answered me, as though I were a pestering child.

"Power, of course. To know oneself, one's limits and abilities, is its own power. To know how one may best subdue another with similar abilities is another."

My heart lurched in my chest. Your words were like splinters of light through the darkness of a tomb, the promise of life in the world outside.

"Another? There are others like us, my lord?"

You hadn't mentioned others. You spoke of us as though we were the only two creatures like us in the known world, like we had been hand-picked by fate to meet.

"There are never only two of any species. Consider how I sired you, Constanta. You have experienced first-hand how we are born."

"Does that mean I could sire another?" I said, pressing my hand to my abdomen in shock. An old habit, associating birth with a womb. But it wasn't childbirth I had in mind.

You gave me one of your surveying glances.

"No, little Constanta. You are too young; your blood is too weak. It would take a thousand years for you to even be able to make an attempt. It's a weighty power, siring. Best to leave it to those who can manage the responsibility."

My head was swimming with so much new information, crowded with questions the way your study was crowded with the baubles you had picked up on your travels.

"That means someone sired you, then," I said, racing

to keep up. "If you're looking for our originating principle, you were made just like I was. Where is your sire now?"

"Dead," you said, dismissing my question with a wave. "He was not as kind as I am. I was his slave in life and he sired me to be his eternal servant. He did not live long after that, unfortunately."

Your irritation was manifest now, warning me to mind my place. I was there to ornament your home and soothe your mind, not bludgeon you with questions. So I gathered my skirts in my hands and stood quietly while you narrated your instruments, your studies, your small discoveries to me. Feeding me tiny tidbits of what you believed I was ready to know, a crease of annoyance still written between your brows.

You always hated it when I overreached the carefully drawn limits of my knowledge.

Probably because you so enjoyed dangling the promise of revelation just out of my reach, the way sailors dangle kippers to make cats dance for their supper.

uestions. I had so many questions, and I should have asked them all. I should have worn you down like water dripping away at a rock until I learned everything you knew. But you must understand, I was only a girl. I was alone, and I was scared. I had no home left to speak of.

It's easy to hate myself for my ignorance now, when I have the hindsight of centuries behind me, but in those first years I was only concerned with surviving. And the best way to survive, I believed, was to surrender myself to you with total abandon and adoration. And God, how I adored you. It went beyond love, beyond devotion.

I wanted to dash myself against your rocks like a wave, obliterate my old self and see what rose shining and new from the sea foam. The only words I had to describe you in those early days were *plunging cliffside* or *primordial sea*, *crystal-cold stars* or *black expanse of sky*.

I dove down deep into your psyche, turning over every word you gave me like a jewel. Looking for meaning, seeking out the mysteries of you. I didn't care if I lost myself in the process. I wanted to be brought by the hand into your world and disappear into your kiss until we two could no longer be told apart.

You turned a strong-minded girl into a pulsing wound of need.

I never knew the meaning of the word *enthralled* before you.

ur first visitor to the home was our last, and although it still feels like treachery, I can't help but admit that I still think fondly on our young harbinger of doom. Maybe it was because I hadn't spoken to another person in decades, possibly even a century by then. I had grown starved for the sound of a human voice that wasn't just the gargled screams of the victims you brought home to teach me how to kill. By then, I was better acquainted with the jugular vein, the forearm's tender ulnar river, and the beckoning femoral artery hidden in the soft cushion of a thigh than I was with pleasant conversation.

That's why I was so startled by the knock on our door that came one heady summer evening. The sun had barely set and I was still sleep-grogged, but I pulled on my dressing gown over my chemise and hurried down the main stairs. You were nowhere to be found, so I stepped into my role as mistress of the house and opened the door.

He shuffled into the dim of our home, a figure wrapped

in stiff oilcloth. The hem of his robes dragged along the floor, smearing dirt through the entryway. Most notably, he wore an eerie mask under his wide-brimmed black hat, long-beaked in the Italian style and battered as though it had been dragged through a warzone.

"Can I help you?" I asked, unsure of what else to say. He was neither pilgrim nor beggar, and certainly not anyone from the village below. He smelled of strange waters, drying herbs, and the slow rot of disease. The scent of sickness quickened my heartbeat, inflaming deep-rooted self-preservation instincts. Vampires learned to fear the smell of infection early on in their second lives to keep them away from meals that might putrefy in the stomach. We don't die of disease, but infected blood makes for foul meals.

The stranger inclined his head at me politely.

"I seek the lord of this house, my lady."

"He is not available."

The words were an easy, set script you set out for me early in our marriage. I was to turn all unexpected visitors away. No questions asked.

"I'm afraid my business is very urgent. Please."

Your voice filled the empty space of the hall, commanding without needing to be raised.

"He's permitted, Constanta."

I turned to see you at the top of the stairs, tall and beautiful and terrible. I was always most impressed with you when I saw you through the eyes of others, beholding you as though it was the first time. You descended the stone steps with a painful, slow deliberateness, not speaking until you came to a stop right in front of the visitor.

"Speak," you said.

The stranger bowed at the waist, polite but perfunctory. He was used to dealing with gentry, but also used to haste.

"My lord, I've come on a matter of great urgency. I am a physician of—"

"Take that off," you said, gesturing to his mask. "If you're going to address me, do it properly."

The stranger faltered, hand raising partway to his face before dropping again.

"Sire, it is a protection against sickness, a tool of my trade. It keeps away the miasma."

"There is no miasma in this house, nor any sickness. Do either of us look sick to you? We're the only ones here. Take it off."

The doctor hesitated, but he did as he was told, unfastening the leather straps that held the mask in place. It came away in his hands, showing that the beak was full of dried flowers. Little bits of mint, lavender, and carnation spilled around his boots.

He was younger than I had guessed, bright-eyed and ruddy with cheeks that still had the fullness of childhood on them. He couldn't have been more than twenty, with curls of brown hair that wanted for a trim. Were it not for the determined look in his eyes and the bruised shadows beneath them, he would have looked perfectly cherubic.

The sharp sweetness of lavender wafted over to me, along with the enticing spice of his blood, heightened without the mask to protect him. You undoubtedly ordered him to speak to you barefaced to assert your power, but also because it would be easier to snap his neck this way, or dig your teeth into his tender throat.

"I am a physician of the body, trained in Rome and dispatched to Bucharest," he said, voice a little quieter now that he was face to face with you. He had to look up to speak. "I have served in fine houses and in the hovels of the least fortunate, diagnosing illness and administering medicine."

"Very impressive. But what business have you with me?"

The boy swallowed. There was real fear in his eyes. But not of you.

"I've come to deliver news of a sickness, spreading like wildfire throughout the region. The doctors of Bucharest can barely move fast enough to fight it, and we've done everything we can to prevent the spread. I am very sorry to say we have not been successful. The illness has reached the outlying cities. Your city, sire. I saw five cases today alone in the town just beyond these walls. I asked for a letter to be dispatched to you post-haste but no one in the town would . . ." He swallowed, unsure of how to proceed. "The people are, ah, superstitious, and . . ."

"They think me a baby-slaying devil," you supplied, with a cordial smile that made it sound more like an introduction. "I'm well aware. As I said, we do not receive many visitors. The situation must be truly dire for you to come yourself."

The doctor clutched his hands around the staff he carried.

"It is . . . grave, I will say as much. I thought you, as the region's sovereign, deserved to know. I'm not sure what relationship you have with the smaller towns, but the people speak of you as their lord. I have found, in times of plague, that if a ruler moves quickly, sometimes catastrophe can be averted."

A thin smile touched your mouth. A cat pleased with the fight a mouse was putting up.

"And what would you have me do, as ruler?"

"Leverage your power to spread the word. Tell the people to avoid the open-air markets and the cesspools, the garbage heaps. They mustn't breathe the foul air; it will infect the body. Those who succumb must be strictly sequestered in their beds."

You gave a dismissive wave, already turning from him. I stepped forward, poised to show our guest out the door.

"Those people do not answer to me. Let them rally themselves."

The doctor took a few strides towards you, and I almost thought he might catch your arm as though you were a common merchant. Bold, this one.

"You have such vast wealth and resources, sire. The people would look upon you as a savior, a benefactor, if you came to their aid. Surely it would only cement their loyalty; it serves your ends as well. You said yourself that it is only you and the lady in this vast home. Perhaps a wing could be donated to the doctors and the nuns who tend the sick, or even a gatehouse."

"Are you sure you aren't a holy man come to lecture me on the sins of excess? It's Constanta you must plead your charitable case to. She's the only one in this house afflicted by piety."

"I was educated by monks," the doctor muttered. "They have their points to make. But I would not presume to ask you to sacrifice your own comfort, only to spare what little pleases his lordship—"

"We're done here," you said, flicking me a subtle gesture that meant I was to dismiss him. "Good day to you. Do not call again."

I gathered my skirts and opened my mouth to see our guest out, but anger overtook his good sense and his tongue.

"You would not feel the same if you could see what was happening to your people," the doctor snapped. "Boils that arise mysteriously and then fester and blacken within hours; children vomiting blood while elders lose their noses to gangrene; healthy young men struck dead in a day! Do not think your stone walls will protect you from this plague, sire. You must make preparations."

You froze, shadowed by one of the stone arches of our home.

"Boils?" you echoed.

"In some cases, yes. Or swellings, rather, on the neck, under the arms, in the groin—"

"Will you come into the study?" you asked suddenly, eyes lit with a strange, urgent fire. The doctor and I exchanged a shocked look at your sudden change of temperament, but you were insistent. "Please. I wish to hear more of this plague."

"You heard my lord," I said, ushering our guest into the darkness of the home. He walked without protest, but his mouth was tight. Suspicious. He was too smart for his own good.

We led him into the cramped room where a desk and parchment were stored, virtually abandoned. You knew how to write, more languages than I had ever heard spoken, but we did not have much occasion to communicate with anyone.

"You said you were educated in the monastery?" you asked, retrieving what little wet ink was left. "Write for me, then, a list of the symptoms. Start from the outset all the way to death; do not spare me the details."

The doctor took the quill hesitantly, casting a wary glance my way.

"So I may watch for the signs of disease in my subjects," you added, smooth as the wax pooling around a guttering candle.

The young doctor nodded firmly, happy to have a task of merit before him. He scrawled out a meticulous list while you loomed at his side, one hand braced against the desk as you read over his shoulder. He seemed so small standing next to you. I was struck once again by the knowledge that he was little more than a boy with a little medical schooling under his belt and the world weighing him down.

"The symptoms don't always progress in the same way, but they set in quickly. Sometimes the rubbing of a cut onion on the sores discourages festering, and I've seen success with a potion of Four Thieves Vinegar as well. But there is no perfect cure, sire, and many die before treatment can be administered."

"Interesting," you muttered, plucking up the paper. I could hear in your voice that you had no interest in the cure, only in the disease. The doctor watched, baffled, as you took in every detail, running your fingernail down the page as you noted them. I drifted closer, sensing a subtle shift in your mood.

A tide had turned. You had come to some sort of conclusion.

"Who in the village knows that you're here?" you asked, not glancing up from the paper.

"No one, sire," the doctor said, and my stomach muscles clenched. An honest boy, then. A fool. "I came alone, of my own accord."

"Good," you said, setting down the paper and smiling at him. "Good."

You were on him before he had time to scream, ensnaring a handful of his hair and wrenching his head back to expose his throat. Teeth tore through flesh like a needle through silk, and you held him fast while you drank deep of him, ignoring his wheezing and gurgling. A torn trachea, then, fast-filling with fluid. His mask dropped to the floor, spilling flowers at your feet. Blood trickled down his neck onto the blooms, and my mouth watered at the tangy scent of iron.

I was well-acquainted with violence by then, but my stomach lurched all the same. I thought you would let him live. Or maybe I hoped for it.

You shoved his jerking body away onto the desk, cleaning your mouth with a lace-trimmed handkerchief while he gasped like a fish wriggling on the hook.

"Drink, Constanta. You'll need your strength."

I stood with my fingers white-knuckled into the skirt of my dress, watching the boy bleed out slowly. His suffering was an enticement, but as much as I wanted to lap at the pool of blood growing on the desk, there was a question burning inside me that took precedent.

"He's their only doctor," I managed, stomach growling. "Without him, the people will succumb to the plague. Why must we kill him?"

"Because he's too clever to live, and too troublesome. The moment the villagers hear that he went to plead their case to the heartless aristocrat, the moment they all start to die and no help comes from the hills, they will turn on us. They'll raid this manor even plague-addled and half-dead; if they think draining my coffers will save them. I've seen it before."

The doctor clapped a shaking hand over the hole torn in his neck, blood trickling through his fingers. He cast pleading eyes to me, his mouth forming soundless words.

"There's life in him yet," I said. "He may still live."

"Not after what he's seen here. Finish him, if you want to eat tonight. There'll be no time to stop to feed on the road."

"On the road?" I echoed, almost a yelp. The room started to spin, faster and faster. I was so hungry all of a sudden.

"We're leaving," you announced, already out the door and striding up the stairs. "Tonight."

I choked back the tears and hunger rising up in my throat. Then my resolve broke. I made a small, miserable sound and hurled myself onto the still-breathing body of the doctor. I latched my mouth around his reddened wound and held fast as he convulsed and thrashed beneath me. Hot blood flooded my mouth in smaller and smaller spurts until finally, he lay dead across the table.

I scrubbed at my mouth with the hem of my sleeve, tears stinging my eyes, and then left the room so quickly it was almost a run. Bloodstained flowers crunched to dust under my feet.

Upstairs, you threw our belongings into a few large chests. My shoes, my dresses, my sewing needles and hairpins. All packaged up tidily like they were being taken to market to be sold.

"Go untie the horses," you ordered. "Bring them around to the carriage."

You always kept a pair of strong black mares, and would replace them throughout our lives with animals that looked exactly the same. As much as you thrived on innovation, you preferred your own domestic life to stay unchanged.

"Why are we running?" I asked, still a little bleary from my fresh meal. A full stomach of blood always made me want to curl up and take a long nap. "We don't catch illness or die. You told me. We're safe."

You stopped what you were doing and took a deep breath. Then you looked at me, your eyes so dark and haunted I nearly recoiled.

"I've seen this before. Plagues come and go and they come again, Constanta. They are one of life's great constants. We will not succumb to the sickness, but trust me when I tell you we do not want to be here when it overtakes the city. You do not want to see what happens to civilization when half its population is dying in the streets."

I brought my hand up to my mouth instinctively, as though to ward off the miasma.

"Surely, not *half*—"

You slammed the lid to the trunk, snapping it closed with brisk efficiency.

"I was only a boy when it happened in Athens. But I know my own mind, and I couldn't forget what I saw after another hundred years of life, a thousand. We're leaving. Finish packing."

We fled by night, in a creaking carriage stuffed full of our most valuable possessions.

hose years are a dark smear across my memory; everything feels blurry and hollow. Plague drains not only victims but whole cities of life. It freezes trade, decays parishes, forbids lovemaking, turns childrearing into a dance with death. Most of all, it steals time. Days spent boarded up in sickhouses pass in a swirl of flat gray. Plague time is different, it stretches and looms, and I confess I can recall little of the decades we spent rushing from town to town, taking uneasy sanctuary until sickness came battering inevitably at the city gates.

But eventually, the plague burned itself out. We were able to stay in cities for longer periods of time, and I stopped tasting the sickly tang of disease in the blood of all my victims. Eventually, it was time to choose a new home, to put down roots and build our little empire of blood and gold once again.

Your discerning eye fell upon Vienna, and so to Vienna we went.

ienna was a whirl of color and sound to my provincial mind, and she was kinder to us, all in all, than Romania had been. We rang in the shining newness of 1452 together, one of the few dates I remember clearly. The city was celebrating an Austrian emperor of the Holy Roman Empire, and reveling in her political and mercantile prowess as a major trade hub.

You bought one of the fine townhouses in the market square with the gold I could never quite trace or keep track of, and filled it with all the modern comforts money could buy. I was suddenly awash in the city, with dressmakers and maids and jewelers and butchers at the tips of my fingers whenever I wanted them. They were called to the house to measure me for gowns or deliver finely crafted furniture and they left as quickly as they came, though my heart never stopped fluttering when there was a knock at the door.

I had become so accustomed to your company that I had forgotten how much it thrilled me to walk among humans, but Vienna brought me back to life. I could see it in my mirror, a new shine in my eyes, the ghost of a bloom in my dead cheeks. It was like falling in love all over again, only instead of falling for the lord of death, now I was in love with the seething, shouting mass of life outside my home. I took to waking up early so I could perch in bed, safely out of the stinging light lingering through the windows, and watch the people of the city hurry home for their evening meals.

You were not impressed by the children shrieking through the streets, or the washerwomen calling to each other in the town square at all hours. You only had eyes for the university, and spent long hours haunting the lecture halls with your notebook in ink-stained fingers. I'm still not sure what you studied: maps or abacuses or corpses drained of blood so you could appreciate them with a clear head. But you slipped out at dusk to catch as many evening classes as you could, and you came back with a line of deep thought furrowed between your brows.

We hunted together in those days, your tall figure following me as closely as a shadow through the tight alleyways. The whole city was our hunting ground, and there were meals aplenty in the darkest corners of Vienna. You preferred pretty women with stars in their eyes, or young men you had dazzled with your intelligence in one of the students' drinking circles. But I had never outgrown my thirst for vengeance, and I preyed on only the most wicked members of society. Men, all of them, who I caught spitting at beggar children or grabbing a working girl's arm so hard it bruised. I reserved a special sadism for serial violators and batterers. In my mind, I was God's lovely angel of judgment, come to unsheathe the sword of divine wrath against those who truly deserved it.

You mocked my lofty aspirations, cynical as ever.

"We are not arbiters of justice, Constanta," you said after I left an abuser's body slumped over and drained in a cesspool. A magistrate, well known about town for skimming off the top of his ledgers and dragging his wife through the house by the hair when she displeased him. "When will you give up this ridiculous crusade?"

"It isn't ridiculous to the woman who no longer has to cower in fear of him, I'm sure," I said, taking your offered handkerchief and wiping off my mouth.

"Will she not be left penniless without her husband's income to live on?"

You were in one of your contrary moods, and I did my best to ignore it.

"And it isn't ridiculous to the poor who will no longer be threatened with destitution now that he's dead."

"You will have the poor with you always; is that not what your Christ says?" you said with a sneer.

I recoiled. An unexpected harsh word from you was as jarring as a slap from any other man, and your temper had been spiking more and more recently. Vienna made you irritable as much as it made me blossom. I wouldn't realize until later that you were irritable *precisely* because I was in bloom, because there were suddenly so many sources of joy in my life apart from your presence.

"Why shouldn't I take my meals where I please? You certainly do. So many young minds cut down in the promise of youth—"

"Are you criticizing me?" you asked, deathly quiet. You were suddenly very close, looming over me in a way that usually made me feel protected, but was now having an entirely different effect.

I staggered back a step, my calf banging into a low crate stuffed with rotting cabbage.

"No. No, of course not," I said, my throat tight. It was a scared girl's voice, not a woman's.

"Good." You reached for me, and suddenly your eyes were gentle again, your voice slippery and sweet. "Don't look so grim, darling. Let's seek some fresh diversions. There's a traveling show in town; would you like to go see it?"

A smile broke across my face, uneasy but delighted all the same. I had been taken by a voracious passion for theatre since our move to Vienna, and was always straining to see bits of morality plays through whatever crowd we found ourselves in. But you had no patience for "common" entertainment, and always complained that humans had lost their flair for the dramatic arts after the fall of Athens. A colorful traveling show lit by firelight was exactly my idea of a night well spent, but I doubt it even ranked for you.

"Yes, I'd like that very much."

You smiled magnanimously and put your arm around me, leading me away from my victim and towards a night of fire-eating and fortune-telling. I was enthralled by the grace and talent of the performers, but I couldn't help but cast a nervous glance to you every so often. In the shifting firelight, there were moments when you didn't even look like yourself. There was a darkness in your eyes and a tightness to your mouth I hadn't noticed before—or perhaps hadn't wanted to.

There are other shadows across the bright spot in my memory that is Vienna. I didn't realize, then, how deep your contempt for human companionship ran. There was an embroiderer who came by the townhouse to stitch intricate designs into the hems of my sleeves and the bodices of my dresses, a bright-eyed young woman near the age I was when you had claimed me. Hanne had an airy laugh, dark skin, and tight curls of hair she always wore swirled up into a coil. She was clever and lovely and could create entire landscapes from tiny stitches of thread.

We enjoyed each other's company during our time together, and I started inviting her to the house more and more frequently, always coming up with some pillow or chemise I wanted her to decorate at the last minute. We shared stories and secrets and plenty of laughter while she worked. I would go out of my way to fix her plates of cheese and apples even though I had started to lose my taste for mortal food by then. I think I could have loved her, if I was given a chance.

"Who was that?" you asked crisply one day after she had left. I was watching her go from the parlor window, admiring the way her green cloak swirled around her feet.

"Hanne?" I asked, startled from my reverie. Surely you knew her name, and her trade. You had been in the house every time she had visited, locked away in your basement laboratory or upstairs reading in our room.

"And what is Hanne to you?" you said, spitting out her name as though it were a curse.

I recoiled, pressing my back into the fine needlepoint of my chair.

"She is my . . . embroiderer? My friend, she—"

"You have fallen into a shameful infatuation with a weak human girl," you snapped, sweeping across the room. You snatched up a pillow she had covered with daisies and a songbird, sneering at it. "A peddler of fripperies."

You tossed the pillow down on the divan next to me, slightly harder than was strictly necessary.

"Where is this coming from?" I asked. My heart was beating a jig in my throat, my breaths coming fast and shallow. I felt like I had missed a crucial turn in our dance.

"You wish to run off and live a rustic life with her in her hovel, is that it?"

"What? No! My lord – I would never – I love you! You and only you have my heart."

"Save your breath," you said, swinging from enraged to exhausted. Your shoulders slumped, your knit brows going soft and pitiful. You looked very sad all of a sudden, as though reminded of some half-forgotten tragedy.

I pushed tentatively up from my chair, crossing the room to you.

"I would never leave you, my love. Not for the entirety of my second life." Your eyes were wounded, filled with suspicion, but you let me reach out and press a gentle hand against your chest. "I swear it."

You nodded, swallowing back more words that threatened to bubble up and betray you. But betray what? Was there some secret heartbreak in your past that you carried in tormented solitude?

"Did something happen?" I asked quietly. I felt suddenly very useless, as though there were depths of pain within you that even my gentle love couldn't plunge. Scars that you would not allow me to see, much less heal.

You heaved a sigh and smoothed a hand over my cheek, taking me in with those appraising eyes. Then, as though making up your mind, you leaned in and kissed my forehead.

"It's nothing, Constanta. Forgive my temper."

With that, you slipped away, leaving me confused and alone.

You left for two days after that. I still don't know to where. You gave no warning, no explanation, simply took up your hat and slipped out of the house one evening while I was still waking up. I dimly remember seeing your dark silhouette stalking away across the city square, shoulders hunched. You gave no indication of when you would be back, and once it became plain that you hadn't simply stepped out for air or an errand, the panic began to set in. I hadn't been without you for a single day since you found me, and I realized with shattering terror that I had no idea who I was if you were not at my side.

Were you dead, decapitated in the dirt somewhere? I didn't know exactly what could kill things like us, but you had theorized decapitation could do it.

Had I done something wrong? Had I earned your total abandonment with my dalliance with Hanne, with my wandering eye for the city and her charms? I ruminated over my every indiscretion, chewing my nails bloody and wandering aimlessly from room to room. The city called to me, and I was desperate not to be alone, but what if you came back and found me gone? Would I have failed another one of your mysterious tests, proving my fallibility? I sent away the artisans when they came knocking at the door, even my precious Hanne, who I never spoke to again. To do so, I felt, would be a betrayal of you.

For two days, I burned. I broke into a cold sweat like I was flushing opium out of my system. I writhed in our marital bed, sheets sticking to my sallow skin, as misery crawled along my body with scorching fingers. I prayed to God to crack open the sky and douse me in enough rain to stop me smoldering, but I was left alone in my sickly fever.

Then, late in the evening on the second day, you arrived at our door. You stood in the doorway, the shoulders of your coat speckled with crystal rain, your cruel mouth reddened from the cold, looking more perfect than ever before.

I sank down at your feet and cried until I was empty,

my long hair covering your shoes like a mourning veil. You didn't pick me up until I was shaking, then you drew me into your embrace and wrapped me in your cloak. You smoothed my hair and shushed me, rocking me like a babe.

"It's all right, my jewel, my Constanta. I'm here."

I held you tight as life, and let you scoop me up like a doll and carry me gently into our bedroom.

ou seemed to me a fire burning in the woods. I was drawn in by your enticing, smoky darkness, a darkness that still stirs memories of safety, of autumn, of home. I touched you the way I would touch any other man, trying to make my eager presence known and inscribe some sense of intimacy between us. But it was like grasping at a flame. I never penetrated to the burning heart of you, only came away with empty, scorched fingers.

Whenever we were apart, you left your essence caught in my hair, in my clothes. I scented the taste of it on the wind, I shivered and ached for it. I could think of nothing but you the entire time you were gone, until you returned to me.

I was happy to spend countless lifetimes chasing the warmth coming off you, even though the haze was clouding my vision.

I still wake to the smell of smoke sometimes.

e made Vienna our home until war, my old enemy, came to the city in the early 1500s. Suleiman the Magnificent sent his gleaming ranks of Ottoman soldiers to seize the city. Their brightly colored tents encircled the city for months, unbothered by the cold rains of fall. Vienna was torn between the Hungarians and the Austrians, an attractive jewel to any expansion-minded ruler and a more valuable bargaining chip by far. Seemingly overnight, there were hundreds of thousands of troops outside our city, and emissaries being sent to negotiate a surrender.

The energy in the city was one of abject dread. Rumors flew about Turks digging under the city, and we could hear the distant detonation of explosives by night, rattling the thick defensive walls.

Religious fervor whipped the churches into a frenzy, and I often heard people talking in hushed whispers about the end of days when I slipped into the chapel to pray in the evening. My piety was a sporadic, half-feral thing, sometimes lashing out at God with teeth bared, other times nuzzling against His loving providence like a kitten, but prayer steadied me. Whether I was talking to myself or something more, it brought me peace.

The world we had all known was drawing to a close, it seemed.

You did not fear the Ottomans, not their weapons nor their foreign ways. You admired their tactical skills, their finely crafted armor, and spoke highly of their customs to me behind closed doors, the way you might talk about the Swedes or the French. You had lived too long to fear one culture more than another, and you had seen more empires fall than I could fathom even existing. War and desolation were par for the course, and so was the inevitable rebuilding and cultural flourishing that came after.

"Perhaps Vienna will remake herself if the city falls," you mused once, watching frightened citizens hurry by outside our windows as the encroaching army drew closer outside. "Perhaps she will become a flower of art, or a trading center worthy of her position."

You did not seem concerned with the human toll such a remaking would demand.

As the trade routes in and out of the city were choked out by the Ottomans, Vienna's tables became more and more meager, but you and I feasted nightly. Chaos ruled the streets, and people were so preoccupied with their own concerns that they were willing to look the other way if someone went missing. There were more young people roaming the streets, restless and wound up with fighting instincts. You welcomed them with open arms, even brought some of them into our bed to toy with before you took your fatal bite.

We grew fat and happy in the city's discontent, and you quietly began pulling your money out of Viennese ventures and cashing out your investments in gold. Another move was coming, then. There wasn't much time left.

My killing sprees grew bolder, more indiscriminate. The frantic atmosphere covered my tracks and allowed me access to men whose disappearances would have otherwise been thoroughly investigated. I went after magistrates, keepers of the peace, wealthy merchants, degenerates all of them. I ripped the throat out of a man who had violated his own daughter, then left a whole month's worth of the allowance you gave me at the foot of his daughter's bed. I ran a war profiteer through with one of the swords he so happily sold to both sides, then delicately supped from his wrist in his smithy. It was like sitting at my father's knee as a child, cozy in the glow of a blacksmith's fire while I enjoyed my simple meals.

It wasn't a vendetta now; it was a purge, my last-ditch effort to cleanse the city of the wretches who haunted her dark corners. I would not leave Vienna in their clutches. Despite the way you turned your nose up at my nightly vigilante activities, my heart was steadfast. Why else would God allow me to fall into your hands if he did not want me to use my monstrousness to serve the common good?

I began to say goodbye to my beloved city, going for

long walks at dusk to try and catch a bit of her color, see a few of her inhabitants before night fell. I was in love with every cobblestone, every bridge, every butcher's boy and flower-selling girl. Vienna seemed to me a perfect encapsulation of the wonder of city life, and I shuddered to think she may fall.

Either way, you and I wouldn't be there to see it.

We fled under cover of night, through an underground tunnel known only to a few. I ran with your jewels sewn into my dress, with hidden pockets to hide silver and gold. We abandoned everything in the townhouse: my fine dresses and shoes; Hanne's lovingly embroidered pillows; your scientific equipment in the basement. We would rebuild even better than before in our new home, you told me.

We were stopped a mile from the city by a band of Ottoman soldiers patrolling the borders of their camp. They brandished their spears, but we made short work of them. We left their bodies in a heap on the ground, blood seeping through their clothes, a spear sticking up out of one of their chests.

"Where are we going?" I panted, struggling to keep up with you in my heavy dress. I thought I might collapse under the weight of it, even with my growing preternatural strength. The night was moonless, and I trusted your night sight better than I trusted mine.

"There's a coach waiting. I paid off anyone who mattered."

You pulled me along by the wrist, almost dragging me

when I slowed too much. We scrambled through the weeds, the distant sound of explosions battering Vienna's walls urging us along.

"And then?"

"Spain. One of my associates is expecting us."

Another explosion sounded, loud enough to rattle the ground under my feet, and I gasped and rushed forward. Sickness, age, and a simple knife wound couldn't kill creatures like us, but I wasn't sure that being blown to bits wouldn't.

The coach was waiting just as you said, with faceless hooded men waiting with two identical black horses. They were the kind of rough folk whose loyalty could be bought for a week or two, highwaymen mostly likely.

You opened the carriage door for me and held out your gloved hand.

"My lady," you said.

I let you help me inside and pressed myself against the side of the coach, my face an inch from the window. As we took off with a lurch, I watched the city shrink to nothing behind us.

From such a great distance, the faithful torches burning along the outer wall made it look like Vienna was on fire.

PART TWO

e traveled by coach for days, drowsing in the sunlight hours and passing our time with quiet conversation or solitary activities by night. You became more withdrawn the closer we got to the Spanish border, referring to notes and letters you kept tucked into your datebook over and over again. I wanted to ask who exactly it was we were going to meet in Spain, but I would have been met with one of your gentle rebuttals, or worse, a flare of your unpredictable irritation. I had learned by then that it was better not to ask about your plans, since I didn't have a say in them anyway. Better to ride along as your quiet, beautiful consort, taking notice of everything and everyone without making any demands of you.

I knew we were going to pass a few nights with one of your many correspondence partners, a Spanish noble of some prominence who had dazzled you with their cutthroat political philosophy.

"Like a modern Machiavelli," is all you had murmured, half to me, half to yourself as you reread the letters.

I never expected *her.*

agdalena insisted on receiving you the instant you arrived, and she was waiting for us outside her manor, flanked by her staff. She was one of the most striking women I had ever seen, with a fine-featured face of cutting cheekbones and a soft, thin-lipped mouth, framed by a confection of black curls. Her light brown skin was set off by a high color through her cheeks. Rouge, probably, despite its impropriety for someone of her station. She was dressed in black satin trimmed with crimson silk, and her dark eyes flashed like twin daggers when she saw you, a smile breaking across her face.

She was utterly, wrenchingly gorgeous. I felt my heart tumble down through my ribs and hit the ground.

"What is this?" I whispered to you, suddenly terrified.

You tore your eyes away from her long enough to bring my wrist up to your mouth and press a kiss to my skittering pulse.

"A gift, if you want it. And a few days of reprieve among high society if you do not. You know I love you, Constanta, don't you?"

"Another woman," I said, betrayal thick in my throat. "You've been keeping another woman."

"Don't be ridiculous. I've been carrying on correspondence with a dear friend, one who is very eager to meet you. I would never discard you, Constanta."

"But you would collect us, like baubles?"

You grimaced, straightening your cuffs and reaching for your hat. Outside, the servants were deftly unloading our coach. We only had moments together before we were thrust into the scrutinizing gaze of high society, silenced by the demands of decorum for only God knew how long. The entire visit, perhaps.

"You've never complained about my trysts before, nor have I complained about yours."

"We hunt together," I corrected you. "We take lovers together, or find bedmates to amuse ourselves for a few hours alone. They have never been *affairs*."

"And neither is this. Nothing untoward has been going on between Magdalena and I, and I'm frankly surprised by your suspicions. You sound paranoid, Constanta. You need rest. Let our hostess show you the best of her hospitality and then decide how you feel about her."

I stiffened at your familiar tone, wondering how long she had been "Magdalena" to you, if you murmured her name devoutly to yourself as you read over her letters full of strategy and policy and blood. I knew nothing about this woman except for her reputation as an iron-fisted ruler, and her appreciation of your insight into the control and rulership of local provinces. I didn't even know how you came into contact with her. Just another one of the many details of your life you guarded jealously, forbidding me the indecency of a simple inquiry.

"We'll discuss this later," you said, more gentle as you kissed my temple. "Put on a smile for the staff and do your best to be civil to our hostess. She may surprise you yet."

I was not permitted another word of argument, because the doors were opening and the thin light of a crescent moon was streaming in. You had timed our arrival perfectly, just at the moment the sun disappeared over the horizon.

I swallowed hard and accepted your hand as you helped me out of the carriage. As we walked arm in arm towards Magdalena, I felt like I was the favored child being presented with an adopted sibling she never knew she had. My head was hot and swimming with thoughts. How long had you been speaking so intimately to this woman, and what did she know of you, of us? Were we to be friends, or was she a prospective victim? Is that what you had meant by "a gift, if you want it"?

My flurry of thoughts came to a screeching halt as Magdalena dropped in a low curtsy in front of me, close enough that I could feel the swish of her skirts. She was smiling at me, her pupils wide and delighted, but her eyes kept flicking over to you.

"My lady Constanta," she said, her voice rich and musical. "I have heard so very much about you. It's my pleasure."

I bowed to her in return, stiffly. She was greeting us both like equals, although you no longer carried your old title of nobility. Who exactly did she believe you were?

"The pleasure is mine, your excellency. Although I'm afraid I haven't heard much about you."

I shot you a look, pure poison on ice, and you smiled back at me tightly. That would earn me a reprimand later, but you would not raise your voice to me in the presence of others.

"My lord . . ." Magdalena said, turning to you. Her voice faltered. Of course it did. I knew very well what she was seeing for the first time: crow-black eyes above a strong, imperious nose and a mouth shaped like a declaration of war. The only thing that ever prevented you from looking fearsome was the amused sparkle in your eyes, more present now than I had seen in years. The hollow at the base of Magdalena's throat fluttered as she took in an unsure breath, then she lowered her eyes and dropped into a perfect curtsy.

It tortured me, how perfect she looked. I wanted to pull her behind the carriage and drain her dry.

"I'm going to direct the servants," I muttered. I grabbed my skirts and tramped over to the coach, where Magdalena's staff were passing my trunks and parcels between themselves. I made a show of ordering them around, knowing that at least I was allowed this luxury in Magdalena's home, and did my best not to look back at the two of you. Ultimately, I wasn't able to manage.

I glanced over my shoulder just in time to see you bring

Magdalena's gloved hand up to your mouth and press a lingering kiss to her knuckles. You clutched her hand close to her chest and said something softly, too quietly for me or any of the staff to hear. Magdalena's lips parted in soft surprise, her eyes gleaming.

I wanted to crawl between whatever was blossoming between the two of you and live there. This was my home too, I wanted to shout. I had earned my right in your bed and I hadn't been consulted on inviting somebody else in, no matter how beautiful she was.

The servants skittered around with downcast eyes, working as efficiently as a hive of bees. I didn't have to spend much time directing them, and soon I found myself back at your side, looking into Magdalena's bright eyes. The fabric peeking through the slashes in her sleeves and the stiff ruff at her throat were as white as death.

"My honored guests must have a tour of the manor," she announced, and clapped her hands briskly. "Then, dancing and dinner."

The servants scattered like a school of fish, running this way and that to throw open doors and make preparations. I had never seen a household so efficient. You arched an impressed eyebrow at Magdalena and she smirked back demurely.

I already resented the rapport I felt growing between you two. I didn't know if I wanted all of your attention, or all of Magdalena's. I was slipping fast into a heady, dark maelstrom of jealousy and want. I needed a glass of water, and a quiet room to sit down in and wait for the world to stop spinning. But there wasn't time. I was swept along on your arm, Magdalena trotting along on the other side of you like a sharp-toothed terrier.

"The home has been in my family for five generations," she said as the heavy wooden doors swung open and ushered us inside. "It is my responsibility and pleasure to maintain it."

I could hear the glow of pride in her voice as I took in the lovely tapestries and the strong gray stone walls, but there was a strange twinge in her words that almost sounded like bitterness. Perhaps the pleasure came with some sort of price.

Servants scattered as she strode through the home, keeping their eyes fixed firmly on the floor, or on the folded linens in their hands.

"You have them so well-trained," you noted, leaning down over to Magdalena although your voice carried easily.

She practically glowed with self-satisfaction.

"Like many of my contemporaries, they were not accustomed to receiving orders from a woman untied to any man, but diligence and a strong hand breaks all bad habits."

The two of you shared a private smile, probably remembering something in one of your letters.

"You've found cruelty to be an effective tool," I said airily, following her through the vaulting wood and stone halls of her ancestral home. Magdalena threw a look to me over her shoulder, quirking a plucked eyebrow.

"I am firm, my lady, and I understand leverage. The people only call me cruel because it is easier to think of a woman as cruel than competent. Surely, you can understand that?"

She was clever, and I wanted to smile, but I swallowed down the treacherous gesture. Let her be clever, and pretty besides. I must not let her ingratiate herself to me when she was obviously already so ingratiated to my husband. Perhaps inappropriately so.

Inappropriate. The absurdity of the word struck me and I almost scoffed aloud. What, if anything, in our life was not inappropriate? We killed to live, we lied and cheated and took lovers, we slipped from town to town like ghosts, draining the populace of their money and blood before moving on. Not a month ago we had brought two young men home with us from the streets and taken our pleasure with them before draining them dry in our marital bed. I had given up *appropriate* when I had given up my ability to eat mortal food, to walk abroad in the sun.

Then why did my heart twinge whenever you looked at her?

I prayed that we would have a moment alone before dinner. To fight, to reconnect, I didn't know. I just needed you without pretense, in private. But I was not to get my wish.

We were separated and ushered into different rooms to dress for dinner. The style had been looser on the streets of Vienna, but now I was dressed in the Spanish style, in severe, dark fabrics with jewels at my waist and a ruff at my throat. The aristocracy were merciless when it came to their airs and graces, you had told me, and would not hesitate to mock or excommunicate anyone who didn't take propriety seriously. I was to be on my best behavior, to remember all you had taught me about high society and keep my mouth shut when I could not.

And so, before I even had an instant to catch my breath, I was laced into a confection of brocade and ushered into the belly of the beast.

The ballroom was filled with twenty or thirty members of the gentry. Her contemporaries, she had called them. They drifted through the ballroom in silk and velvet, drinking from beaten gold goblets while a quartet of musicians strummed on lyres. I suspected some had traveled in for the festivities.

How long had Magdalena been expecting you? Since before the siege on Vienna? And moreover, why did she want to impress you so badly?

I found you among the crowd, looking handsome and impassable in your black doublet and jerkin trimmed with gold. I sank into my place on your arm, suddenly feeling exhausted. The night had just begun, but I wanted to curl up and sleep it all away.

"You look lovely," you said, smoothing your knuckle over my cheek as though nothing was wrong, as though Magdalena didn't exist. For a moment, under the scorching weight of your unadulterated attention, I felt like I was the only person in the world.

Maybe it wouldn't be terrible, a treacherous thought offered, to share you with another if you still looked at me like that when we were alone.

Magdalena was leading the dance, a prim and provincial series of turns and bows. She darted in between her partners, lightly brushing hands and shoulders in a complex series of touches. Every so often, her dark eyes flickered over to you.

"Dance with me," you said, already leading me out onto the floor. I didn't protest. I was happy to have something to do with myself instead of gape at the proceedings like a fish swimming through strange waters. I held your hand lightly and let you lead me through the first steps of the dance, quickly correcting my form by watching the gentry whirling around me. The world was a swirl of skirts and feathered hats, moving faster and faster as the musicians picked up speed.

Even surrounded by the flowering beauties of Spain, Magdalena's loveliness was undeniable. She cut through the crowd like a shark darting through shallow waters, her teeth bared with laughter. She never missed a step, and never stayed with one partner for long. Every inch of her, from the soft curve of her cheek to the sharp line of her jaw, tormented me.

"Do you want her?" you asked, the words almost snatched away by the whirl of the crowd.

"What?"

We came back together, your hand a vise around mine. In the golden light of the hall, your eyes burned. I only ever saw that fire in your eyes when you were on the precipice of devouring something. It was all expectation and want.

"Do you want Magdalena for your own? To be your companion by day and warm your bed by night?"

Jealousy slithered up my throat as quick as a snake. But there was some other emotion mingled in, dark and sweet. Desire.

"Do you?" I asked, skirts snapping around my ankles as you twirled me. The whole world was turning, tilting on its axis.

"Ours is a solitary existence. It would be good for you to have a friend. A sister. I have never forbidden you from taking lovers, Constanta. Remember that."

You made it sound like a gift, a gentle reminder of my own freedom. But I heard your double meaning: *do not deny me this.*

I opened my mouth but the words faltered. I didn't know what I wanted. My heart, whipped into a frenzy by the wine and the dancing and the gleam of Magdalena's dark eyes, felt torn in two directions.

I never got the chance to answer you. We were pulled apart by the demands of the dance. I was sent spinning into another man's arms while you crossed to Magdalena, slipping in beside her as close as her own shadow. No one could deny the light radiating from her face when she looked at you, like the halo of gold on a holy icon. Her cheeks were flushed pink from the vigorous dance, tantalizing proof of the hot lifeblood pulsing just beneath the surface of her skin.

How can I blame you for wanting her, my lord, when I wanted her so badly myself?

I strained to see over the shoulder of my partner as he turned me in dizzying circles. Older than me, handsome, with a healthy tan on his brown skin that told me his blood would taste like ripening summer apricots and the dust of a well-traveled road. I barely saw him, barely registered the appreciative smile on his face.

All I saw were you and Magdalena, two lovely devils indulging in a little human revelry. Your hand fit perfectly into the curve of her back. Her elegant, sloping neck invited admiration as though she already knew what you were, as though she were teasing you.

You lowered your mouth down by her ear, lips brushing the lobe as you spoke, something private and urgent. A slow smile spread onto Magdalena's face as she clutched you closer. What were you telling her? Our secret? Or a more carnal proposition?

My feet faltered over the demanding steps of the dance, and I broke the tight circle of my partner's arms. He tried to coax me back, the cadence of his Spanish insisting that there was nothing to be embarrassed about, that we should try again. But I brushed him off, took a few staggering steps further onto the dancefloor. The couples whirled past me like exotic birds winging by in a flurry of feathers, and my stomach clenched. I felt like I was slipping out of my own body and floating above it, observing myself as a spectacle.

Then there was a small touch on my arm and I turned

to see Magdalena, smiling that wry smile at me with her hair coming loose from its elaborate styling. There was a bloom across her chest, a slight sheen of sweat gleaming at her hairline. She looked like she had just stepped out of an opium dream, all blown pupils and reddened mouth.

"Your excellency," I breathed, my heart suddenly in my mouth. "You will forgive me. I do not know the steps of this dance."

Moving with shameless deliberateness, Magdalena cupped my jaw in her hand and kissed me full on the mouth. Not the light touch of a friend's kiss catching the corner of my lips, but a kiss full of intention and warmth. My head swam as though I had just emptied a whole glass of wine, the entire frantic room falling away. It only lasted an instant, but by the time she pulled away, I was completely inebriated.

"Then I shall teach you," she proclaimed, and took my hands in her own. "Do you want to lead? Or shall I?"

I stammered foolishly, throwing my eyes wildly around the room.

Magdalena threw her head back and laughed, a beautiful wolf savoring the terror of a rabbit.

"Me, then. It's as easy as breathing. One foot and then the other. And don't overthink it." We moved together across the floor, fluid and unified. If any of her subjects had seen the kiss, they hid their disapproval well, restraining themselves to gossiping behind spread fans. No one stared or reeled in shock, merely continued with their dancing and drinking, eyes politely averted. As well-trained as her servants, then. This must not have been the most scandalous behavior they had seen from Magdalena.

"You must never overthink any good and pleasurable thing," Magdalena went on, her cheek almost pressed to mine as we twirled. The wine on her breath was as sweet as blackcurrants. I wanted to taste it on her lips as much as I wanted to taste it in her veins. "We should never deny ourselves any pleasure in this life."

I could almost hear you in those words. Had you coached her? I wondered. No, there hadn't been enough time. Maybe she really was a soul after your own likeness.

We glided together until the song was done and then, out of breath and giggling from our exertion, raised our hands in applause with the rest of the crowd. The musicians bowed, mopping sweat from their foreheads.

Magdalena tucked her arm in mine and led me with deliberate steps through the crowd, leaning over conspiratorially.

"You must sit with me tonight at dinner. I must have you close, Constanta. I want us to be the best of friends."

You waited for us at the long wooden table, already seated at the left of Magdalena's chair and making a show out of nursing a glass of grenache. I doubt any of it actually passed your lips. I still had some of my taste for food and drink then, as the undying life hadn't yet entirely bled them of their pleasure.

Magdalena poured me a double measure of wine. Her crow-quick eyes watched my every movement, following the glass as I raised it to my lips, and you observed us both like one of your experiments. Trying to look disaffected, of course. But I knew the gleam that came into your eyes when something seized your attention.

"Try the *polbo á feira*," Magdalena said. "It's a peasant dish, but one I favor, and my kitchens make it better than anyone. You've got to dunk the octopus in boiling water a few times before butchering it; that's the secret to keeping the meat sweet."

I obligingly opened my mouth for her when she raised up a bite on her fork. The flesh was tender, spiced liberally with paprika and slick with olive oil.

Magdalena beamed, watching me chew with the delight of a child bottle-feeding a kitten.

"Will you eat?" Magdalena asked you, poised to hand-feed you as well.

"I never have any appetite when I travel," you said, plucking the fork from her hands and setting it back down on her plate. You held her wrist between thumb and forefinger, slyly suckling oil off her little finger. If she saw the flash of your sharp teeth, she didn't show it.

"If it wouldn't be rude for me to ask," you began, leaning in closer, "how is it that one as beautiful as yourself is not yet married? I'm sure it's expected of a woman of your station. Ever since your father disappeared . . ."

A look of pure glee came over Magdalena's face, and she dropped her voice to a conspiratorial whisper.

"I think I shall never marry, my lord. I will simply take lovers and never let any man shackle me with wedding vows."

"Ah, but I'm sure your wealth attracts all manner of little birds hoping to fritter away a piece of it in their nests. You must receive suitors by the boatful."

"Indeed," she said with a laugh. "And I entertain every one. I hear their love poems and their declarations, I accept their gifts and I grant them a private audience, but that's as far as it will ever go. Not that they know that, of course. They sincerely believe they have a chance, poor boys."

You hummed your approval, dark eyes shining in the firelight.

"And if they have hope, they continue to behave themselves and allow you your little indulgences and eccentricities. Very clever, Magdalena."

"A third of the men in this court want to bed me and wed me, another third despise me but won't speak against me because I've carefully collected records of their affairs and murders and misdeeds, and the other third simper and fawn because they know where true power lies, and they wish to ingratiate themselves with it."

"And the women?"

"Ah," she said, her voice almost a purr. She broke eye contact with you and shot me a smirk. "Women are another matter entirely."

Her fingers brushed against my leg under the table, equal parts bold and tentative. I seized her hand in mine, unable to decide whether I wanted to cast her off or pull her closer.

I squeezed her fingers and let her hand go, and she

withdrew her hand into her own lap. But we were seated so closely together we were almost touching, and I could feel the living heat wafting off her body. Her blood smelled strongly spiced and as sweet as fortified wine, shot through with a salacious, irresistible musk.

I wanted to take her away from you and pull her into some darkened hallway, unfasten the lace ruff from around her throat and run my mouth along the pale slope of her neck. I wanted to feel her lifeblood bursting in my mouth, savor every note of her complex bouquet.

Instead, I swallowed through a dry throat and said, "I'm sorry to hear about your father's disappearance."

Magdalena let out a peal of laughter. She was flushed from drinking and dancing, and her shoulders were loose with joy.

"I'm not! I deposed him, Constanta. Didn't your husband mention?"

I shook my head politely, wondering what kind of madhouse I had been brought into. Magdalena threaded her arm through mine and pulled me in closer. I noticed that you were lightly holding her free hand, running your thumb over the delicate bones in her wrist.

"My father," Magdalena began, her lips almost brushing my ear, "was a tyrant. Feared by the people, stubborn in all his strategies, and untrustworthy with the family fortune. I spent my life in his shadow, trying to wrest control away from him, or at least convince him that I could be trusted with diplomatic responsibilities. He didn't see my skill for politics. But I will not accept a world behind bars, Constanta. I must always have my freedom. So I worked my magic with gossip and bribes and carefully exposed secrets, and the next thing you know my father is wasting away of gout in some remote hunting lodge, out of the public eye."

"You banished him?"

"He quietly . . . showed himself out. Barely left a trace. With his reputation ruined there was no life for him here anymore. And that's when my life truly began."

"A wonder," you pronounced, your gaze devouring the bow of her lips, the line of her jaw. "A genius."

Now I understood why you were so enamored with her. She was as cunning as you were, and as cold as a Transylvanian winter. Beneath the fripperies and the giggles there was a girl made of steel, one who would do whatever it took to survive.

You could never resist a survivor. Or a mirror.

You took her hand and pressed an open-mouth kiss to the pulse on the inside of her wrist. The nobles were watching; people could see you. You didn't care.

"And what would you sacrifice, my Lady Machiavelli, for your freedom? What would you give me if it were in my power to promise you total immunity from the shackles of society? A life without limits, without laws to chafe against?"

"Anything," Magdalena said without a moment's hesitation.

"If I could take you away from all this tomorrow, would you let me?"

"Yes."

You smiled against her skin.

"Good."

The rest of dinner passed in a blur. I ate whatever Magdalena hand-fed me, I listened to the warm lull of your voice as she trailed her fingers along mine. I gently touched the curls that had come loose at the base of her neck while you fed her little sips of wine from your glass; she whispered salacious nothings in your ear while her ankle brushed against mine under the table. We grew increasingly entangled, the air between us close and hot, and it was no surprise when you said:

"It's getting late. Will your excellency be retiring soon?"

"I think I shall," she said breathlessly, catching your drift immediately.

"Allow me to escort you to your rooms," you said, standing to pull her chair out for her. She threw a dark-eyed glance through her lashes at me. It was a look men would have razed whole cities to the ground for.

"Will Lady Constanta be joining us?" she asked.

I wrung my napkin tightly in my lap, out of sight, and tried to keep my voice level. I was being invited to bed with you both, and you would be enjoying each other tonight, whether I came or not.

"Later, perhaps. I'd like to take some of the night air first."

"Of course," you said magnanimously, as though you were allowing me some indulgence instead of taking your own. You leaned over and kissed my brow, your hand hovering over the small of Magdalena's back. "I have your permission, don't I?"

You said it so quietly I doubt Magdalena even heard. I nodded mutely. There was no other answer, had never been.

"Good," you said, and disappeared with Magdalena into the darkened hallway.

I didn't stay at dinner long after that, but I wandered the halls for a while before heading to your bedroom. You would be waiting there for me, I was sure, with Magdalena, probably in some kind of compromising position.

God, what was I allowing?

It felt like something that was happening *to* me, but I had agreed to it, hadn't I? Part of me wanted this. Wanted her. I shouldn't be feeling so dismayed.

I walked circles through the drafty halls, trying to decipher my own feelings for a small eternity. But I knew I had to go into the bedroom eventually. The suspense about what I would find, and no small amount of anticipation, was tangling my insides into knots. I steeled my heart and tried to quiet my fluttering stomach as I pressed silently into the darkness of your bedroom.

Magdalena was spread out on top of the sheets, her gleaming skin set off by the dark fabric. One of your hands encircled her delicate ankle, hooked over your shoulder, while the other gripped her ass tight enough to leave bruises. The sight seared itself into my memory.

You were fucking her in our bed.

No. Your bed.

I was only ever a guest, every night contingent on my good behavior.

And Magdalena was behaving for you very well. Arching the small of her back and digging her long nails into your shoulder-blades while you drove into her. She made soft, eager noises, rising and falling like the cooing of a dove. Pretty, perfect Magdalena, with her cheeks and nipples rouged for you like a king's courtesan.

I stepped into the room, silently unpinning my hair as though nothing was out of the ordinary. This was my place, after all, in your room. Nothing, not even the slick circle of Magdalena's panting mouth, could make me feel ashamed to be there.

You kissed her throat, the tender junction of her neck and shoulder, and then spoke. With your lips still on her skin, with your prick still inside her.

"Constanta, I can feel you over there brooding."

Magdalena gave a little gasp, eyes alighting on me as though I were a ghostly apparition. She had been too engrossed to hear me enter, apparently.

I smiled at her, letting my eyes travel over the lines of her body before coming back onto her face. I would know every inch of her. She would not be able to hide anything from me. Not her nakedness, not her secrets, not her designs for you.

"Will you come to bed?" you asked me, breath ragged as you slid in and out of her. Slow, controlled. The way you liked to start. Magdalena shuddered, biting her lip to suppress a little noise. She must not have thought it seemly to moan in the presence of her lover's wife.

I watched her squirm while I unfastened the emeralds from my ears and dropped them onto the vanity. It was difficult not to. She was a cornucopia overflowing with carnal delights. My hands itched to touch her, but I maintained my icy mask.

"Am I to be bidden to my own bed like a dog invited to beg at the master's table?" I said coolly.

You did look at me then, dark eyes erratic with lust and irritation and some other, less pronounceable emotion. Admiration, perhaps. You showed it to me so rarely I hardly knew how to recognize it.

"Constanta," you said, savoring the syllables like they were a filthy note passed under the pews to you in church. "My jewel, my wife."

"Getting better," I said, shucking off my heavy outer dress and draping it over the back of a chair. I loosened the buttons at the nape of my neck and left the length of laces down my spine for your agile fingers to unfasten. My hands were trembling now, my heart beating fast and hot in my throat.

You tilted Magdalena's chin towards me, showing off her pink cheeks, her silken fall of black hair. The desire that had been slowly uncoiling in my stomach reached my chest, tightening painfully.

"Look at how lovely our new bride is," you said, nipping her earlobe. "Come and kiss your sister. Show her there isn't any animosity between you."

Magdalena, ever-willing, held her arm out to me. Those lovely fingers curled, beckoning me closer.

"Please," she said, voice sweet as a berry so ripe it was ready to burst.

I was furious with you. You had manufactured my consent every step of the way, a mere formality. This had always been your design for the both of us; we were always going to end up here, in this bed.

But I was also delirious with want, and half-convinced that you had been right all along. It was so much easier to believe that you always had my best interests at heart.

I swallowed dryly and crossed the room to the bed, running my hand over the curve of your back as I bent down to kiss her.

Her mouth was warm and willing, and when she made one of those soft sounds against my lips, I shuddered. She tugged me down gently onto the bed, forming the shape of that word again before the buck of your hips snatched her breath away. *Please.*

"You," I said, kissing her with more urgency as I allowed you to make short work of my laces, "are a torment."

esire makes idiots of all of us. But you already knew that part, didn't you?

agdalena sighed into my kiss and I knew I would kill for her, die for her, do it all over again and then some. I had never wanted a woman like this, not even Hanne, not to the brink of such total desolation. It reminded me of the way I loved you, and that shook me to my core. One body could not hold such fervor, such feeling, I thought. It might rip me in two.

Your lips sought mine while she was still wrapped around you. I ran my hand down the smooth plane of her stomach, then lower still.

"Can I please?" I asked breathlessly.

Magdalena nodded, and then made a delicious little sound when I circled her with my fingers. She writhed and mewled under our expert ministrations, calling out my name and yours in turn.

Then, at the moment of her climax, you sank your teeth into her neck.

She convulsed and cried out, but she held you fast. As though she were welcoming the pain and the change, not rejecting it. I reeled, my mind addled by pleasure and the scent of hot blood wafting towards me. This was happening too fast, I wasn't ready for this, I wasn't ready to share my life for ever with another one of your wives, I wasn't . . .

You kissed me firmly with blood-slick lips, and then I was gone. You guided my head towards the pulsing wound at her throat, and I sucked the sweet red liquor from her skin while she murmured my name, her hands tangled in my hair. I had never known such perfect tenderness, such absolute ecstasy.

It terrified me.

We shared the wine of her in sips, alternating between drinking from her and kissing her, kissing each other. I could scarcely tell the difference between your two mouths in the dark, that's how close the three of us were.

Magdalena obediently opened her mouth for you when you opened the vein in your wrist, and drank from you with a determined ferocity I didn't expect to see from someone who was not yet one of us. There was a flash of her steel again, as compelling as it was frightening. She would not be made the world's victim, that much was obvious.

My blood wasn't as potent as yours, and I didn't know if it had matured enough to offer the powers we enjoyed, but I opened a vein for her all the same.

We passed the night drinking from each other and making love, taking full advantage of the heightened sensitivities that flooded Magdalena's system. None of the servants bothered us, and none of the dinner guests came looking for us.

They were well-trained, after all. And as Magdalena wound her fingers around my wrists and covered my chest in hot kisses, calling me sister with that mischievous smile on her face, I couldn't help but wonder if I was being trained, too.

We took our leave the following night, our carriages loaded down with Magdalena's finery. She left the manor in the care of one of her highest-ranking servants, promising that she would return sooner rather than later. I wonder if she knew that sooner had a way of becoming much, much later when you lived as long as we did. But she was young, optimistic. Maybe she didn't believe that taking up with you meant the total obliteration of her previous life.

She would learn, in time.

She was vain and petulant and my rival besides, I reminded myself as we headed out into the ochre dusk light together. I was determined to see her worst qualities and keep her at arm's length even as we traveled pressed together in the coach. But she was also brilliant, and beautiful, and so sure of who she was and what she wanted out of the world. She held my gloved hand in hers whenever the carriage went over a bump and she fed me little bites of treacle from her traveling bag and she dozed against me with her mess of curls tickling my cheeks. She thought up word games to keep us diverted, and woke me every evening with a little kiss in the corner of my mouth.

I fell in love with her quickly, even as my head railed against the stupid machinations of my heart.

There was an uncontrollable fire in her that was hard to look away from, much less resist, and the more time we spent together, the more my admiration for her grew. I knew I was lost when I caught myself lying awake dangerously close to dawn in a tavern room on the French border, watching her face while she slept. Every little flutter of her eyelashes fascinated me, and I catalogued the curve of her face as though I had been commissioned to paint her portrait. Even after you stirred awake and pulled me against you, shushing me back to sleep, all I saw in my dreams was her face.

There wasn't much hope for me, after that.

Far from stifling my love for you, my feelings for her simply stoked the devotion that enveloped my heart whenever you walked into a room. Seeing the two of you walking arm in arm through city streets, window shopping and laughing, filled me with an irrepressible delight. You called us your little foxes, and you were our north star, guiding us through the night. My heart fluttered in tandem with yours whenever she shared the latest gossip with us by firelight, and we were both thrilled to hear her thoughts on political developments across the continents.

Magdalena was connected to a seemingly endless

network of informants, rivals, friends, and philosophical sparring partners whose letters found her wherever we stayed. You warned her against too much correspondence with the outside world, against jeopardizing our secret, but you indulged her habits in those early years. It was your honeymoon after all, this grand tour across all the European cities she had always dreamed of visiting. She should be allowed some little indulgences. It was her right as a new bride.

You wouldn't start hiding her letters and discouraging her from answering her aging cohorts until much later, when her novelty had worn off.

We toured Lyon and Milan for decades, taking in the local color with leisure, then eventually spent a winter in Venice at Magdalena's request. You chafed against Venice, its seething color and swirling masses of people, but I reveled in it. The bustle reminded me so much of my Vienna. Magdalena and I never tired of wandering the piazzas, watching the merchants hustle by. We would walk along the thin edge of the canal arm in arm, me listening as Magdalena gossiped about all the city officials and their wives. She knew their families, their position on politics, and which of them were taking bribes, and she had her own opinions about all of them. I marveled at her mind for diplomacy. If only the Great Council of Venice would bend their ears to a foreigner, and a woman no less, they would have a powerful weapon at their disposal.

You were irritable during the whole first winter we

spent in the city, complaining about the noise and the damp and how there was no quiet place for you to carry out your research. I had begun to unravel your fixation on science at that point, your obsession with cataloguing and dissecting the human animal. All vampires find some way to stave off the monotony of an endless life, with hedonism or asceticism or a rotating door of lovers as short-lived as mayflies. You kept your hands and mind busy with your hypotheses, your never-ending research into the condition of human and vampire. Maybe you were determined to be the first person to riddle out what processes transmuted one into the other. Or maybe you just needed a distraction. I don't have to ask from what, my lord. I know the undying life has a certain inevitable weight to it.

"Let's go out," Magdalena exclaimed one night as she tossed her arms around your neck. You were hunched over your desk, peering at samples of flora and fauna from halfway across the world. Why they were of interest to you, I still have no idea.

You gave a smile that was more of a grimace.

"I'm busy, little one."

Magdalena put on one of her spectacular pouts. A well-timed pout from her could probably have brought down the walls of Troy.

"But the opera is tonight! You promised we could go."

"And you can go. Take your sister and give me some peace. I'm very absorbed at the moment, if you can't tell, my love."

Magdalena whined, but I was elated. You were giving us permission to traverse the city alone. Without you ushering us along through the shadows, glowering at passersby, Magdalena and I could make conversation, take our time as we strolled along the rain-slick streets. Venice had been in the grip of Carnival over the past week, the festivities spilling into the streets. The world outside our door was sure to be riotous with sound and color, Venice at her most ferocious and lovely.

"I'll get my capelet," I announced, trying to keep the excitement out of my voice. I didn't want you to change your mind at the last minute and decide we needed our usual supervision.

But in the end, the draw of your research won out, and Magdalena and I were permitted to travel by ourselves, so long as we promised to return before the first light of dawn. You were fond of these paternalistic rules, always circumscribing our freedom with little laws.

Magdalena and I put on our finest gowns and strode out into the night in a rustle of silk and ribbons, our feet leaving wet tracks on the cobblestones.

We giggled all the way to the opera house, so happy to breathe the free air with only each other for company. Magdalena laced her gloved fingers through my own as she pulled me down alleyways and over bridges, and my heart pounded a happy drumbeat in my chest. Tonight, the whole expanse of star-riddled sky seemed to be shining especially bright for us. It was she and I alone, for once, with the entire world at our feet. We could have done anything we wanted to. Caught a boat to Morocco, or passed ourselves off as princesses at one of the lord's carnival parties, or drained a beautiful young thing together in the darkest alleyway where no one could find us. We were drunk on sheer possibility.

We didn't divert from our plans, however, because Magdalena was a devotee of the theatre, and because I wasn't quite brave enough yet to do anything that would get us into trouble with you. A little mischief was one thing; outright subordination was quite another. I didn't want our beautiful evening to be spoiled by your raging temper when we arrived back home.

So even though Magdalena stared hungrily at the masked partygoers in their plumed hats and billowing brocade dresses, I pulled her away from the heart of the revelry and towards our destination.

The opera was one we had never seen before, in the new, more serious style that was starting to replace the sung comedies so popular around the region. Opera was growing in stature and influence, spreading all over Europe, and the composers had begun to experiment, to great acclaim. I've sat through so many operas with Magdalena I can scarcely remember their names, but I remember this one. It was a rendition of the biblical story of Judith. Familiar enough to me, who still read the Bible for recreation and meditation despite your scoffing, but relatively new to Magdalena, who had never cared much for sermons.

"They should have let her fight," Magdalena whispered

to me behind her fan. The lovely Judith onstage lamented her position in Israelite society, desiring to fight back the invading horde alongside her brothers. Moved by the plight of her suffering countrymen, she swore vengeance against the Assyrians. "I would have let her fight, if I was in charge."

I smiled at this. It was hard not to smile at Magdalena when her mind was set on something, declaring her will like a true high-born lady.

"She has her revenge," I said. "Keep watching."

Magdalena reached out in the darkness of our opera box and clutched my hand when Judith welcomed the leader of the Assyrians, Holofernes, into her home. She sang sweetly to him as he reclined on her lap, secure in his safety in the arms of a woman. Then, once Holofernes had fallen into a drunken sleep, she called for her maid to bring her a sword.

Magdalena took a sharp breath, her throat fluttering. I leaned in closer to her, wanting to savor every bit of her pleasure. Through her eyes, I was able to experience the story for the first time all over again. My heart leapt in my throat as Judith sang out her triumphant aria and swung her sword. It came down on Holofernes' neck with a great gush of stage blood so satisfying my mouth watered. Magdalena gave a little jolt in her seat and clapped her hands together briskly, and I laughed and pressed my cheek to hers. Her joy went through me like lightning, catching fire in my chest.

"Who is that woman with her?" she whispered, as the

two women held down Holofernes' writhing body and completed the decapitation.

"Her maid, I believe."

"Maybe they were like us," she said, voice velvety and soft in the darkness. We were still pressed together, her lips near my ear, her eyes fixed on the stage.

"And what are we, Magdalena?" I asked. The question was out of my mouth before I had a chance to weigh it. We had been together for years, the three of us, but there was still no name for the affection between Magdalena and me. It seemed incomplete, somehow, to call her lover or friend.

She turned her face towards mine, nudging my nose with her own.

"Don't tell me you think we're rivals, dear Constanta. Haven't you realized by now that there's enough of him for each of us?"

"I'm not thinking about him," I said, and to my surprise, I was being honest. My head was always full of you: when we were together you overshadowed every conversation, and when we were apart I made myself sick with missing you. But now Magdalena had my undivided attention. "I'm talking about us, you and me. Let's be honest with each other, for once."

Somberness was not one of Magdalena's strong suits, and it was my constant disposition, which resulted in a rift between us. She was content to glide in and out of my bed, teasing me mercilessly one day and then sliding her arms around my neck and calling me beloved the next, and she never saw the contradiction in her actions. I, however, took love much more seriously. Love was no girlhood game. It was an iron yoke, forged in fire and heavy to wear. I suppose I wanted to know once and for all if Magdalena really loved me, even if it was just in her way.

Magdalena looked at me for a long moment, and then deliberately began removing the glove of her free hand. She did it with her teeth, so she wouldn't have to let go of me. Once the gray silk was settled into her lap, she brought her wrist to my mouth. Secure in the dark anonymity of the opera box, I kissed the pulse beating languorously underneath her fragrant skin.

"You are half my heart, Constanta," she said with as much seriousness in her eyes as when she wrote her long letters of political advice. "We have our spats, but that will always be true."

Magdalena brought her thumb to her mouth and bit down, sharply enough to draw a bubble of blood to the surface. She held her hand out to me. Not up to my mouth, as though she were inviting me to taste her, but in front of my chest, as though she were a merchant inviting me to shake hands on an agreement. I understood her right away.

I wrapped my lips around my own thumb and made an identical wound. Magdalena latticed her fingers through mine, our thumbs hovering over each other.

"Let's be sisters," she said. "Really and truly. The kind of bond that no one can separate, no matter how they try. Even if we're on opposite ends of the Earth, you'll have a bit of my blood in your veins and I'll have a bit of yours."

We pressed our thumbs together and Magdalena kissed me hard, her mouth bruising mine as our blood mingled. Warmth spread through my entire body. I felt like I was being transformed from human to vampire all over again; made new in the wake of a powerful love.

"I want to celebrate Carnival with you," I breathed, breaking our kiss.

"Tonight?" Magdalena said. Her eyes were wide and sparkling, delighted by my unexpected whim.

"Tonight. I want to see the city with you, and I want to remember our first Carnival with you by my side."

"But what about—?"

"Never mind him. I'll handle everything when we get back. We'll just say we got turned around and delayed. If we slip out now we can enjoy the city for hours before we have to go home."

"You're serious," she said, a smile bursting across her face.

"I'm serious. Besides, you've seen the best part of the opera now anyway."

We gathered up our things and swept out into the night, following the glow of torches and singing of revelers to one of the large city squares. We stopped at a vendor to buy two of the eerie *volto* masks that were so popular with women at the time before picking up our skirts and speeding off after the rest of the partygoers like young girls. In our winter capes, we were indistinguishable from any other person in the crowd.

We gasped at the fire-eaters and the acrobats, gawked at the ladies of Venice in their elaborate costumes, and let out delighted yelps when men in gruesome masks jumped out at us. I had never seen so much beauty together in one place. My memory of that evening is one happy blur, with the memory of Magdalena's hand in my own clear as crystal. When we finally tore ourselves away from the party and began to race home, dumping our masks and veils into the arms of two young girls who had been watching the festivities from afar with longing eyes, we were as tired as dancing princesses from a storybook.

You were as absorbed in your research when we returned home as you were when we left, oblivious to the secret pleasure we had indulged in away from your watchful eye. With a few perfunctory kisses and kind words, you disappeared back into your world of calculations and hypotheses, leaving Magdalena and me to slip away to bed.

The rooms in Venice were small, and we all shared a large featherdown bed that we girls very rarely had to ourselves. Having Magdalena all to myself was a special delight that I didn't intend to waste.

I kissed every inch of her as though she were a holy relic, sloughing off her dress with the delicate care I might use while unwrapping a communion chalice from its linen. She whispered my name like a prayer as I worshipped the secret place between her thighs with my mouth. Her fingers tangled in my hair and she giggled as I brought her closer and closer to the brink, my own body trembling with desire. She was so beautiful like this, head tipped back, brow smooth and free of any worry. I wanted the moment to last for ever: just her and me trapped in a small, perfect eternity of pleasure.

Lying with her made me feel so vibrantly alive. It was almost enough to make me forget that I was already dead.

aybe I was drawn to her because she was so fully alive. Even your bite hadn't yet snatched the high color from her cheeks, the sparkle from her eyes. I liked looking at her better than I liked looking at myself, for it became increasingly difficult to recognize myself in the mirror. My long reddish hair shined with the illusion of life but was always cold to the touch, even in the sunlight, and my skin had a pallor most women had to paint their faces with white lead solution to achieve. My eyes were dark and flat, more animal than woman, and I often startled passersby because I forgot to remind myself to blink. I wondered if eventually even my reflection would fade away, leaving nothing but the cold unbroken surface of a mirror.

I was a perfect, immovable statue, painfully beautiful but without any of the small graces that mortality bestowed. I looked more and more like you every day.

Even the thinnest rays of sun were painful to me now, and I couldn't frolic with Magdalena in the soft light of dawn or dusk. I was less and less sated by bread and wine, although I sometimes slipped into the church for communion just to see if I could still taste anything at all. The hunger was relentless, my only companion in the quiet moments between travel and conversation about your newest theory of human nature. I took up diversions constantly to fill the void: needlepoint, viola, the rosary. Nothing made me feel full.

So I lived vicariously through Magdalena, all her wide-eyed wonder at the world, all her brutal little firsts. We hunted together, broke the necks of wicked men and drew beautiful girls and boys into our bower for kisses and love bites. Magdalena and I brought these delicate young blooms to the edge of pleasure and pain, taking small, restrained sips from their still-pulsing veins. I suppose we wanted to see if we could do it, feed from someone without giving in entirely to frenzied bloodlust, and we didn't think it was fair that every person we took our sustenance from should die. We fancied ourselves just and fair as we coddled our swooning beloveds and sent them home covered in hickeys and a few barely noticeable pinprick wounds.

You, of course, found out eventually.

"What's the meaning of this?" you demanded, after a boy had stumbled out of our home with his lips swollen from kisses and blood drying on his neck but still very much alive. "You two are going behind my back trying to sire a new family, is that it?"

"Of course not," I scoffed.

"No, no, my love!" Magdalena crooned, wrapping her fingers around your arm. She steered you to the nearest chair. "We would never do such a thing."

"You couldn't even if you wanted to, you know. You aren't old enough; your blood isn't strong enough. Is this Constanta's doing?" you asked, though I had barely even spoken. "She's infected your mind with her moralism."

"I've done nothing!" I exclaimed.

"This is about your obsession with justice, isn't it?" you said, dark eyes flashing. "You think those youths are innocent and so you let them live. Hear me, Constanta: no one on this wretched Earth is innocent. Not you, not me, not those children."

Tears sprang to my eyes unbidden, and I scolded myself. I hated crying in front of you. I felt like it gave you even more power over me, like your heart was an empty lachrymatory waiting to catch my tears.

"Beloved, *please*," I said.

Magdalena, bless her, stepped in before you could reduce me entirely. She settled herself at your feet, skirts pooling around her, and laid her head on your knee. She was the picture of coquettish contrition, but I was beginning to know her well enough to know that it was, at least in part, an act.

We all developed our tricks for dealing with you: my invisibility, her sweetness.

"It was just an experiment," Magdalena said, thinking on her feet. "We were curious what would happen if we let them live, if it could be done at all. You're always talking about studying the nature of humans and vampires. We were simply releasing a few test cases into the wild."

You threaded your fingers through your hair while your gaze burned into my skin, searching me for any sign of disobedience. You usually looked at us like we were hoards of gold, precious and rarefied. But now you looked at me the way you looked at one of your books. Like you were draining me of all useful knowledge before tossing me aside.

"Very industrious," you murmured. Your voice was still suspicious, but you seemed to be willing to accept her answer. For now.

, for my part, tried not to hold against you how you came to love her. You hadn't set out looking for a new bride. You had simply fallen in love, just the same way I had fallen in love when you had presented Magdalena and me to each other. I couldn't blame you for that, could I? I tried not to think of the quiet machinations that had gone into our meeting as we followed the whims of Magdalena's wanderlust from country to country. I tried to banish the clamoring thoughts of how long you must have been writing letters to her without my knowledge or consent, telling her all about our life together. Winning her over to your side.

I tried to be generous with you, my love . . . but the seeds of doubt, once planted, put down deep and stubborn roots. Soon, the suspicion that you had not been entirely honest began to gnaw at me, despite the joy of a life shared with you and Magdalena. I was suspicious, and even more dangerously, I was curious.

Asking you directly was out of the question, and I didn't want to needle Magdalena for information either.

If you found out I had gone behind your back to ask questions about your behavior you would be furious, and I was loath to disrupt the idyllic family life we three had in those early days. Perhaps, my lord, I was simply a coward.

You must forgive me. You had overstepped so many of my boundaries and left me so little of my own privacy that it didn't seem unfair for me to deny you a little of yours.

We were staying in a rented house in the Danish countryside, with a repurposed barn in the back for your workshop. You spent more time out there than you did in your own bedroom. I waited for you and Magdalena to go out on the hunt together before I went looking for your letters. You two loved hunting together, the thrill and the sport of it. You left me to my misguided sense of justice in those days, having given up on converting me to killing for any other reason.

I let myself into the barn quietly, careful not to leave so much as a footprint in the dirt or a fingerprint in the dust. This is where you hoarded all the new inventions flooding the scientific markets, barometers and handheld spyglasses and calculating machines. They were lined up carefully on your worktables. You also had laid out human bones, harvested from victims and hand-washed, and had somehow acquired an entire skull laid out next to a pair of forceps and scribbled notes.

I ignored the evidence of your grisly work and set about searching for something more precious: a simple wooden cigar box where you kept stationery and letters of sentimental value. I had never so much as seen the inside of this box, but I knew it was cherished by you, because I was forbidden from going near it.

My heart hammered at the weight of my indiscretion as I looked under papers and stooped below the tables to rummage through wooden crates. Touching that box was a sin worthy of excommunication from your good graces, I was sure. But then again, I was strictly forbidden from ever entering your workshop unaccompanied. What was one more sin to add to my litany?

I found the cigar box lying out in the middle of the table, carelessly exposed. You never once thought I would have the strength to disobey you, did you? The possibility that my will was stronger than yours never even crossed your mind.

I opened the lid so, so delicately. My reward for my tenacity was sheaves of letters in your tight, prim hand. I flipped through the papers, looking for ones addressed to Magdalena. I only wanted to know how long you had been in contact with her, I swear it. I just needed to know if you had been courting her for years, right under my nose, or if your fascination with her was as recent as you claimed.

I found her letters, my love. And I found so many more.

At first, I was confused. I couldn't read with your lightning efficiency, but I had taught myself well enough to know that there was correspondence here dating back centuries, since before you and I had even known each other. Some of it was written in strange alphabets, in any of the many languages you spoke and I didn't, but there were a few I could decipher.

They were love letters. Written to absolute strangers, stretching across time and space. Strangers that you called husband. Lover. *Wife.*

I recoiled from the box as though I were Pandora herself, pouring woe out into the world. The letters spilled from my hands and hit the table. Impossible. You had never mentioned other spouses. I was your firstborn, your Constanta. I had sacrificed everything for the crown and you had raised me into queenship in return. I was unique in your eyes. Special, even after we brought Magdalena into our world. I was the love that started it all.

Wasn't I?

It wasn't that I didn't expect you to have taken lovers, to have sought out human companionship during the many years you spent wandering the world. But I had thought you had truly been alone, without an equal at your side possessing your same power, your same sweet-edged curse. But you had turned these people, at least a half dozen of them, and the evidence was right there in your own hand. You seduced them from afar and then coached them through first meetings and first seductions, promising whole worlds if only they would allow you to take that fatal bite. You even used some of the same language when you convinced them to take up with you.

A gift.

A life without laws, without limits.

The choice is yours.

You had specifically sought them out: poets and scientists and princesses, all wracked by some recent trauma. There were fire survivors, victims of brutal marriages, starving artists, and wounded soldiers among your ranks. All exceptional in some way, all vulnerable. It made me sick to think of them, to imagine their glassy-eyed faces when you finally appeared and told them you had come to raise them up out of the dirt and into an immortal life of ease. And you had kept meticulous record of all of them, the same way you kept meticulous record of your little experiments.

I hastily gathered up the letters and put them back where I had found them, doing my best to remember their correct order and arrangement. Then I rushed back into the house, letting the door to the barn slam shut behind me.

The awful truth threatened to swell up and engulf me like a wave, and I was almost driven to my knees by the force of it. I was not your first. You had been keeping secrets from me our entire life together.

I swallowed hard and forced these thoughts from my mind.

You were entitled to your privacy. I shouldn't have impinged on it if I didn't want to find out something that upset me.

But try as I may, I couldn't rationalize your lies away.

I couldn't work up the courage to confront you about them, either. At least not at first.

I tried to run away once. Even now, I'm filled with shame at the thought. I wish I could say I broke away from you over and over again, valiantly flinging myself towards freedom. But that would be a lie. I was only brave enough to flee once, and it was on such a petulant whim it could hardly be called premeditated.

It was a dreary English summer night, with rain trickling down from the moonless sky. We were on our second decade in the country, and the two of you still had that honeymoon glow, that sparkle in your eyes when you looked at each other. Most days, that look filled me with warmth, but that night, my heart was cold.

I watched you looking at her in the firelit glow of our flat, your hand on her knee as she bent her head close to yours to show you one of her skillful drawings, and my blood burned in my veins. Earlier that evening you had shouted at both of us for making eyes at the messenger boy who brought you letters from the university, and now you were as sweet as a hen tending her brood once again.

It made me sick, watching Magdalena preen for you. She had always been better at fawning over you when your whims turned dark, and so you must love her better, no matter what you said. If I had given it a moment's more thought I would have realized that I loved you and Magdalena both fiercely, so it was perfectly reasonable for you to love the both of us the same, but I wasn't thinking clearly. I was sick with misery and jealousy, and the confines of the small London flat suddenly felt oppressive.

I needed air. I needed the starlight and the wild throng of humanity outside our door. I needed to feel like I belonged to myself again.

I dashed through the door while you were kissing her, into the dark and the rain without so much as a bonnet on. I had no idea where I was going, I just wanted to get away from the life we had built together, from the cycle of brutality and tenderness. My legs carried me out of habit to the doors of the parish church of St. Saviour's, looming beautifully on the edge of the Thames. I often came there by night to pray, to think, to watch the delectable people come and seek their absolution. Seeking their own scrap of the eternal, which I had in such abundant supply.

Yet, that night, I would have given anything to be a mortal girl once again, flesh dying around me just as quickly as my beauty had come into bloom. An infinitesimal life seemed preferable to an endless one trailing after you like a dog.

I retreated into the darkness of the cathedral, my hair dripping and the hem of my skirt dragging mud across the marble floors. As a girl I had been taught that churches were the dwelling place of God. I used to peer into every tiny shrine and crevice in the cracked walls of our village chapel looking for Him. The priest had told me that God was in everything, in the communion bread and in the cry of newborn babies and even in me. It had made me feel clean as newly fallen snow to hear him say that. But it had been a long time since I had felt clean.

Like Christ, I had become intimately acquainted with violence and the sins of the world, but I had not come away unblemished. Violence felt like holiness to me now. Perhaps I had given something away the night I had first tasted your blood, and now the place inside me where God used to dwell was empty. I hoped not, on that night of all nights. I needed divine strength in my veins. I needed some sense of worth beyond your hard-won approval of me.

Sinking onto a nearby kneeler, I bowed my head and took a shaky breath. I had been praying less and less, and the words of the Our Father felt clumsy in my mouth. But I pressed on, my fingers laced together so tightly the knuckles turned white.

"Please, God," I begged, my tiniest whisper echoing through the cavernous cathedral. "Make me strong. I'm so tired of being weak."

I don't know how long I stayed like that, bent over and reciting a litany of prayers. Darkness pressed in around me like a familiar friend, shrouding my tears and disguising my face from the few other penitents who wandered past. I prayed in silence as they lit their candles, as content with my shadowed corner of the church as a child was in its mother's embrace.

All the sermons equated God with triumphant, searing light, rising in the east to drive away demons and disease. But I wondered if the Creator of the day also dwelled in night, guiding us all in the darkness. Perhaps I had not been forsaken when I made the night my eternal home.

The thought sent a warm shiver through my body, and in that moment I understood the rapture of mystics who burst into tears when they felt the presence of God.

"Constanta," a voice behind me said. I gasped as I was roused from my reverie. For a moment I didn't know where or who I was.

But it was not God who had spoken.

It was you.

You stood behind me in your long cape, holding your hat between your hands. You might have looked apologetic, if it wasn't for the expression on your face. Haughty as ever, but with the telltale signs of restrained fury that I had trained myself to look for. Your lips were drawn tight together, and there was a furrow between your brows.

"I've been looking for you for an hour," you said, in such a calm tone of voice that my stomach quivered. I don't think I had ever seen you so angry. I had no idea what you were going to do, and I was terrified.

Good, I wanted to say. I wanted to spit the word out onto the ground at your feet and watch the shock cross your face. I wanted to cause you a lifetime of inconvenience, dig my heels in the next time you tried to move us, kick and scream when you tried to enforce your curfews. I wanted to fill the cathedral with accusations of every unkind and controlling thing you had ever done to me or Magdalena, and make you answer for them.

But instead, all I could say was:

"I'm sorry."

You held a hand out to me silently. I pushed myself up onto shaking legs and took a few tentative steps towards you. In that moment, I couldn't have predicted what would happen next. You could have kissed me or slit my throat and either would have made as much sense.

Still I walked to you. Slow, obedient steps. I walked when I should have run the other way.

Your hand slid up my neck and your fingers threaded through my hair. Slowly, they tightened into a painful grip, and you tipped my head back so I was looking up at you. Your eyes were entirely dark, devoid of any pity.

"No more running, yes?" you said, voice silky and low.

"No more running," I whispered, tears springing to my eyes. What else could I have done? I belonged to you. There was no world for me outside the range of your watchful gaze, no past and no future. There was only this moment, you holding me like a kitten by the scruff while your own blood coursed through my veins.

You kissed me. Punishingly, until my lips were bruised,

until there was scarcely any air left in my lungs. The force of your love nearly drove me to my knees. I was no woman; I was merely a supplicant, a pilgrim who had stumbled across your dark altar and was doomed to worship at it for ever.

I don't know what I had been thinking, supposing I was strong enough to leave.

he years ticked by, and our honeymoon with Magdalena became daily domestic life as the world changed around us. Pascal, Newton, and Descartes advanced their theories in the world, much to your rapt delight, and the steam engine revolutionized agriculture and commerce. Europe's might grew by leaps and bounds alongside her brutality: the cities got bigger and dirtier, imperial expansion became more widespread, and my corsets got tighter and more elaborate.

By the turn of the eighteenth century, we had traversed so much of Europe that we had seen fine city squares and capital sieges, driven through just as many pastoral scenes of harvest as we had fields razed to the ground by war. The world turned on its axis, ever spinning, ever coming back to where it started, but we did not change. The greatest philosophers Europe had to offer declared that we were in an enlightened age, progressing from rudimentary darkness into elevated civilization, but I had trouble believing them. The constant warmongering of imperial powers and brutal capture and trafficking of human beings were dark marks on any claim to enlightenment, as far as I was concerned.

You remained raptly fascinated by the cyclical rise and fall of the human animal, drawn like a hungry wolf to empires limping along on wounded limbs. And Magdalena remained adamant on corresponding with the greatest minds of any century, trading letters with kings and courtesans and court philosophers. Her intellect was unparalleled, and she craved the stimulation of advising on political matters. Edicts and coronations were like chess pieces to her, and she had an uncanny ability to predict how one head of state would respond to another's treaty. She seemed to find a sense of purpose in these exchanges, and would sometimes write so many letters in a day that she would pace through our rooms dictating her thoughts to me while I wrote them down for her.

But she was never permitted to meet any of these luminaries. You were suspicious of anyone who tried to get close to her. Jealous, Magdalena and I agreed privately. We would never say it in front of you, of course, not wanting to risk rousing one of your dark moods. Magdalena had seen plenty of those by then as well, been left by you on a busy street corner when she said something that offended or been berated when she tried to argue about why she should be allowed to hunt alone. You kept her close at hand always, insisting it was because you loved her, because you wanted to protect her and couldn't stand to be without her.

As someone who had been loved in this way for centuries, I also knew it was much easier to keep an eye on someone who was close at hand, to guide their mind and direct their steps.

You made it into an art form, this quiet sort of violence. You were so far into our heads your gentle suggestions so often felt like our own thoughts.

And for a long time, Magdalena simply thought that there was no use in keeping up correspondence with great minds that would only shrivel and die in a blink of our immortal eyes. Gradually, she retired her stationery and stopped accepting letters. We kept moving, never staying in one place long enough for our nature to be discovered by the locals, but we stopped following her adventurous whim from nation to nation. We traveled by your compass now, following the northern star of your interests. Just like it had been before she came to join our family. And Magdalena, poor lovely Magdalena, began to fade.

It started with the fatigue, with the long bouts of bone-deep tiredness that had her sleeping not just through the day but through most of the night.

Her melancholy was palpable, wafting off her like the sticky-sweet scent of death. Soon she lost interest in any of her favorite diversions, even in hunting. I had to take her by the hand and tug her out of the door with me at night to convince her to feed. I once saw you bring a crystal glass of fast-chilling blood to her lips the way you might feed a child, just to get her to eat. You murmured to her in Greek, a language that sounded arrestingly tender and intimate to my ear, and urged her to find the will to get out of bed.

I would lie in the dark next to her on bad days, smoothing her dark curls and humming to her snatches of the songs my grandmother used to sing to me. Sometimes she would smile at me, or cry. Other times, she simply looked past me as though I wasn't even there. Those were the most difficult.

"What's wrong, my darling?" I asked quietly on a particularly bad evening. Two days prior she had been on top of the world, giggling at your jokes and preening in the mirror and stalking the streets like a beautiful panther out to find her nightly prey. She had been ablaze, barely needing any sleep and so full of ideas that she could scarcely string them together into a sentence. But now, she could hardly bring herself to brush her own hair.

"You're acting as though you have no interest in living anymore," I whispered, my voice breaking.

Magdalena looked at me with empty eyes.

"I want to live," she whispered back. Probably too afraid that you would hear from your rooms next door. "But I want to live *in* the world, not on the outskirts of it. The days just go on and on, Constanta, they never change . . . I'm tired."

We did our best to learn to live with Magdalena's melancholy, which seemed over time to become a fourth person in our marriage. She would be her usual efferves-cent self for days, sometimes years, but the melancholy always came back, calling on her like an unwelcome old lover disrupting a wedding.

You determined that moving so often was agitating her distraught mind, so we settled in Berlin at the sunset of the nineteenth century. The newly established German empire was in full flower, with the Kaiser presiding over a capital city stuffed with factories and theatres. The sprawling city center was large enough to hold even your attention for a number of decades, full as it was of wealth and slums, criminals and extraordinary scientific minds, all moving together in a great human sea. You were able to dig your talons into the city's soft underbelly every night, and Magdalena was able to divert herself with German opera, Parisian revues, and Russian ballet performances any time the darkness started encroaching on her brain. It worked, for a little while. But even a life of perfect leisure was not enough to soothe her desire for true freedom. She wanted, above all, a life unshackled to convention or even the people she loved, and so her light began to dim once again.

Once, Magdalena slept for days, waking only in fitful spurts to refuse water, refuse food, and whimper to be left alone in the darkness. But on the third day, she pushed herself up in bed and called for blood. You slaughtered the prettiest of the servants for her, offering up our household's beloved fatted calf. Eventually, the color came back into to her cheeks and the strength flowed through her limbs once again. She returned to us as though she hadn't been walking the knife's edge of destruction days ago, smiling that starry smile.

Your fears, however, were not put to rest.

"She needs to see a doctor. A psychiatrist, something. She needs treatment, Constanta. To be brought under control."

You were pacing the living room, fuming and fretting while Magdalena slept in your bed. The fatigue was coming for her again, and you feared what would happen when it had her completely in its clutches.

"She's sick," I said, as mildly as I could manage, keeping my eyes on my embroidery. I wanted to advocate for her, but I also wanted to avoid your wrath. You had been good-humored for a time after you brought Magdalena to live with us, but now your temper was getting shorter and shorter again. "She doesn't need to be brought under control; she needs the right medicine."

"And what medicine might that be?"

I flicked a quick glance up to you, and then down at the French knots I was stitching.

"Fresh air. A bracing walk around the city by herself."

"When she's not distraught, she's agitated and restless. I take my eyes off her for a moment and she gets into trouble; she can't be trusted."

"Equally sharp minds to correspond with," I went on, swallowing my fear. I had to ask, for Magdalena's sake. I had to. "A friend that isn't also a lover."

"What does she need strangers putting foreign ideas in her head for, turning her against our kind? She has us both, she has power, she has the world on a platter. She should be grateful."

Your voice had the thin insinuation of a threat in it, and my blood went cold at the sound. My mind rushed back to those letters I had found. So many other lovers who had simply disappeared off the face of the earth, wiped clean from your memory except for a few mementos.

Had any of them been sick like Magdalena, losing their shine when they could no longer dote on you and smile for you every hour of the day?

"Is that what happened to the others?" I said, before I could stop myself. This conversation had been festering in the back of my mind for years, and I could scarcely believe it was truly happening now. But here we were, at the awful climax of so many smothered arguments. "Were they not grateful enough for you?"

I bit off the words in a fit of anger, a thousand tiny slights bubbling to the surface in one foolish, reckless moment. As soon as the words were out of my mouth, my muscles seized in terror. God. What had I done?

You turned to face me slowly, bafflement and anger written equally across your features.

"What did you say?"

I opened my mouth but no sound came out. My practiced stitching stuttered, and I stabbed my thumb with the needle. I barely felt it, I was so scared.

"Did you go through my things?" you asked, crossing your arms. I was suddenly aware of how tall you were, of how small I was by comparison.

I shook my head rapidly, my embroidery abandoned in my lap.

"N-no, I don't know what you mean. I just . . . I assumed there were others. Before us. You've lived a very long time, my lord."

You stared at me for a long time, weighing me like gold that you suspected was little more than painted tin.

"There were others," you pronounced eventually.

The words went through me like an electric shock. I had all the evidence of your past love affairs I needed, but to hear it straight from your lips . . . It wasn't the loving that made me sick; it was how much you had hidden from me, and for how long.

"What happened to them?" I asked, my throat dry. If I had come this far, I might as well ask the question that haunted me at night. There was no unsaying what I had said and I would hate myself for ever if I fled the conversation now. "Where are they now?"

"Fled or dead," you said, eyes glittering dangerously. Your arms were still folded across your chest like a child being reprimanded by his governess, but your jaw was set like a warrior ready to strike. It always amazed me how you could play victim and aggressor at the same time.

"Who killed them?" I asked, my voice barely louder than a whisper. For a long moment there was silence, broken only by the ticking of the faithful German clock in the living room.

You crossed the room to me in long strides, and for a horrible, impossible instant I thought you might strike me. But you went down on one knee instead, taking my wounded hand in your own and fixing me with your heaviest look.

"You're young, unschooled in the ways of love. Love is violence, my darling; it is a thunderstorm that tears apart your world. More often than not, love ends in tragedy, but we go on loving in the hope that this time, it will be different. This time, the beloved will understand us. They will not try to flee from our embrace, or become discontent with us."

You brought my thumb to your mouth and suckled off the blood, as gently as a mother might bandage her child's bruised knee.

"Love makes monsters of us, Constanta, and not everyone is cut out for monstrosity. My other lovers went mad, they railed against me and rebuffed my affections, they endangered our lives with foolish trysts with humans and they betrayed my trust. They had to be put down, my love, like a horse with a broken leg. It was a mercy. I swear to you. Do you understand?"

I nodded slowly, every appendage heavy and numb. I could barely breathe. *Put down*, you had said. Like an animal.

You swept a strand of my hair behind my ear and rubbed the line of worry from between my brows, rearranging my face into a picture that pleased you.

Then you took my jaw in your hand and squeezed so hard that tears sprang to my eyes.

"Good," you said, your voice suddenly dark. "Now stay out of my room."

That was your final word on the matter. You left me alone in the living room, shaken and on the verge of tears. I pressed my hand to my mouth to smother a shriek of horror. I knew then I was truly trapped with you, and any pipe dream of running away was nothing more than a flight of fancy. If I ran, you would track me down, and you would do to me what you had done to those other husbands and wives. I shuddered at the thought, sobs threatening to tear out of my chest.

I was shackled to you by iron bonds, and so was my darling Magdalena. There was no way for me to wriggle away without damning her to your anger, and so I resolved to stay. To watch and to listen, and to wait for a perfect moment sometime in the future where Magdalena and I could breathe the free air together.

ou ushered us out of Berlin quickly after that, as though the whole city had been spoiled by Magdalena's continued illness. She sat at the divan and stared out the window, sallow and wan, as you ordered the house to be packed up with utmost expediency. I found myself powerless, wringing my hands while you brooded and Magdalena languished and strange men took my paintings down from the wall. I had no idea how to help either of you. The best I could do was quietly crawl into Magdalena's bed and nuzzle her nearly-comatose form for an hour or so each day, and to sit with you as you took your fill of the morning news, listening to you read interesting headlines aloud. Neither of you would be consoled back into a smile. So, I learned to be content with my own company, to not take Magdalena's every dark mood as mine to fix. She had an illness, the doctor you hired had said. A feminine hysteria resulting in listlessness and ennui.

I thought, perhaps, it was simpler than that. I thought that she was simply fading the way flowers denied sunlight droop and die. Magdalena lived for her freedom, and with it taken away from her, life lost its luster.

You never were able to give her her beloved freedom, since letting her roam freely was strictly against the design you had for our lives. But you were able to augment her joy for a time with a force so powerful it may as well have been the sunshine and free air she gave up to be one with you. A force of pure, unfettered joy.

I just never expected to have to travel all the way to the cold reaches of Russia to find him.

PART THREE

lexi, our sunlight, our destroyer. My prince cast in marble and gold. We could have endured a hundred years more, clinging to each other even as we tore each other's throats out, had it not been for Alexi. He was the antidote to our miseries, a short-lived splash of sweetness in our bitter lives. With Alexi in the mix, our household knew levity again. At least for a short while.

He was as inevitable as a revolution, and heralded in just as much violence.

It was summer in Petrograd, in the heady October of 1919. The Tsar had been shot dead by the Bolsheviks only a year prior, and the vast Russian empire had fallen into civil war just as rebuilding efforts had begun to get underway. The nation wrestled with itself, struggling to define itself in a fast-changing world hurtling towards an ever-shifting destiny. But, despite her wartime scars and explosive temper, Russia was still a beautiful, mysterious ideal in your mind, the source of so much of your beloved philosophy and literature. You wanted to study the intricacies of all the political schools and systems battling for dominance. You believed that strife brought the soul of mankind to the surface of society, and you wished to chart the height and breadth of it for your studies.

"Are you sure it's safe for us here?" I asked as we stepped off the steaming train. The Petrograd station was a swirling watercolor of browns and brass, echoing with the shouts of newspaper sellers and merchant women.

I breathed in the scent of the city deeply. I tasted hot bread, oiled machinery, and the tang of fresh blood ground into the cobblestones. This was a city on the edge of self-realization, or of dissolution. No wonder you were drawn irresistibly into her milieu.

You cupped my face in your hands, your silhouette wreathed like a devil in brimstone smoke by the steam pluming from the train.

"We've waltzed through a hundred tiny apocalypses, you and I, walked unharmed through the ash of countless crumbling regimes. We feast on the ruin of empires, Constanta. Their destruction is our high feast day."

I pressed my lips together. Where you saw glorious progress, I only saw war, famine, and desolation. Humans had learned in recent years to make machines so ferocious they could blow a person to bits, vampire or no. I wondered if we should be more concerned about the way the world was tilting.

Magdalena emerged from the train, squinting against the thin dawn light. We would have to hurry to our apartments for a long sleep before the sun was at its full height. You kissed her gloved hand.

"Say hello to your fresh start, my love."

The apartments you rented us were near the city center, optimum for hunting. I wish I could remember more about them, but we weren't in Russia for very long. All I can clearly recall is the beautiful crown molding rimming the room Magdalena and I shared, tiny flowers rendered in swirling white plaster.

It was an autumn disappearing fast into a frosty winter, with the last rain-battered golden leaves still clinging valiantly to the trees. Still, we spent most of our time out of the house, attending night markets and visiting whatever theatrical performances were still running. The city was too dangerous for Magdalena and me to walk freely without a chaperone, you said, although I couldn't fathom what terror any human could unleash on us that we weren't fully prepared for. You urged us to stay at home, to read Pushkin and sew and practice our music, while you frequented the coffeehouses and taverns. You trafficked with radicals and constitutionalists, anarchists and Decembrists and representatives of the Duma, cataloging them with rapt fascination. Such a vibrant symphony of human philosophy and desire on display, you said. Such a roiling brew of ideas, of potential.

Potential. You always loved that word. You were drawn to potential like a shark to blood.

Magdalena all but seethed with jealousy over your political connections, and begged you to inform her over every new coup, each philosophical principle. You doled them out the way you would candy to a child, smiling warmly at her as you teased her with your knowledge, all the while forbidding her from taking up correspondence of her own. It was too dangerous for a woman, you said.

Unsurprisingly, Magdalena and I became restless. I could not resist the siren song of a new language, a new culture to explore, and Magdalena was itching for fresh air and fresh ideas. She privately referred to our time in the apartment as her "gilded confinement", and more than once I had to talk her out of letting herself out onto the street. I wanted to let her go. I wanted to turn my back while she slipped out the window, or throw the door open wide for her the moment you disappeared from view. I wanted her to taste freedom, to feel the salty sea air toying with her hair, to find a lover or a meal in a darkened tavern. She was still young, still fresh and vibrant. I feared smothering the light that came back into her darkened eyes when she dreamed of roaming the whole of Petrograd.

But, my captor, I feared your ire more. So I coddled her and shushed her and kept her shut up in our stuffy home just the way you wanted, without you even having to ask me to.

You must have known, my lord. You always knew. You could sense the moment one of us began to draw away from you with the acuteness of a bloodhound. That's when either the iron fist or the velvet glove came out.

Sometimes it was both. But ever since Magdalena's melancholy became more pronounced, you favored sweetness. Magdalena was delicate, you confided to me. Prone to emotional weaknesses and flights of fancy. We must handle her carefully for a while, give her everything she wanted. I didn't want her to run off and abandon our family, did I? I didn't want to lose my only friend. Best convince her to stay then, by whatever means necessary.

I didn't realize what means you were referring to until you took us to the artist's studio. He was a favorite of yours, lauded in the coffeehouse for both his progressive politics and his mastery over stone, plaster, and oil paints.

"A true savant," you declared as you helped Magdalena into her coat. "A genius of his age. I must show you some of his work. Anything you want in the studio, you can have. Pick whatever beautiful thing strikes your fancy and we'll bring it home."

At the time I thought you were just in one of your magnanimous, indulgent moods, the ones that made your kindness feel extravagant. I should have learned by then to expect some kind of scheme.

The artist's garret was squashed between two tall buildings, accessible only by a narrow set of stairs. Inside, the close air smelled of plaster and silk flowers, and a fine dusting of white powder clung to Magdalena's and my skirts as we walked. The walls were crowded with blank canvases and half-constructed wooden frames, with chisels lying about haphazardly on tarps. It was like entering the harried mind of the artist at work, untidy thoughts and all. Magdalena and I stopped to admire every bust, every painting, but you strode on ahead, eyes keen as though searching for something in particular.

"Chin a little higher, please."

A man's voice, distant yet close. The artist, perhaps?

"Show me imperious," he went on, and I heard the soft tapping of a paintbrush against a pallet. "I want to see the arrogance of Alexander."

You ducked behind a sheaf of cloth draped across a doorway, moving towards the sound of the voice. Magdalena and I followed, stepping lightly to avoid pots of paint piled up on crumpled newspaper.

The artist stood wrapped in a tattered smock, taking in his subject as he compared life to the fantasy he was creating on the canvas. The subject in question was a young man, golden-haired and lovely, with sea-blue eyes and a full, mischievous mouth. He stood stripped to the waist despite the frost on the windows, holding up a platter of fake fruit and doing his best not to shiver.

"I'd feel more imperious if it wasn't as cold as the devil's tit in here," the model said in a musical tenor.

I looked at you. You were observing Magdalena, who was looking at the model. Desire, as faint yet undeniable as the light thrown by a single candle, flickered across her face.

I swallowed and folded my hands primly in front of me. After living with the both of you for so long, I knew trouble when I sensed it.

"Ah, my friend, you've made it," the artist crowed,

clapping you on the back. The gesture startled me. I couldn't imagine someone speaking to you so familiarly, but you seemed at ease around him. Perhaps acting the congenial comrade was one of your new personas. You spun whole personalities out of silken promises to get close to whoever you needed to. It was one of the reasons you were able to keep us alive so long, and one of the reasons I sometimes woke with a start in the middle of the day and stared at you, wondering who I was sharing a bed with.

"Who are these lovely doves you've brought?" the artist asked, stroking his graying beard as he looked at Magdalena and me with a twinkle in his eye. Not leering. Friendly. Truly happy to see you and to see us. I was impressed, if a little concerned, at your ability to convince a being you saw as little better than breakfast that you two were bosom friends.

"My wife," you said, extending your arm and pulling me in close. "And my ward, Magdalena. Her mother drowned in the Spree last spring, very tragic."

I resisted my urge to roll my eyes at you, and Magdalena nearly managed it.

You delighted in making up stories about Magdalena, whether you claimed she was your ward or your daughter or your widowed niece or your sister in training for the convent. But I was always your wife. I think you categorized us this way less to elevate my station above Magdalena's—we were both your wife behind closed doors—and rather because no one would believe I was anything but a matron, a spoken-for woman. Magdalena said I always radiated a faint sense of motherly worry.

"Of course, my friend," the artist said with a chuckle. "Of course."

I had no idea whether he believed you, but I saw that it didn't matter to him either way. A true libertine, then.

"I'm freezing, Gregori," the model complained. "Either tell your handsome friend and his ladies to take a seat while you paint or give me back my coat."

"Mind your manners, Alexi," the painter grumbled. He shot a sidelong glance to you as he picked back up his brush and palette. "These young actors, they're all the same. Heads as big as the moon. Please, sit."

He gestured to a few mismatched folding chairs and we sat, Magdalena looping her arm through my own. She squeezed gently as Alexi resumed his post. Back arched, neck angled gracefully, eyes shadowed by thick lashes so blonde they were nearly transparent. He was one of the most beautiful men I had ever seen. And he couldn't have been more than nineteen.

Desire and foreboding curled together in my stomach.

We watched in patient appreciation as the painter worked, you occasionally pointing out some lovely piece of statuary in the studio to Magdalena, who nodded her approval. Your eyes kept creeping back to Alexi, however, in tiny flickers that would have been invisible to someone who didn't know you as well as I did. You stole glances at him like tiny sips of wine with dinner, and he did his best not to color under your gaze. When he caught your eyes with a disaffected toss of his head calculated to look natural, the electricity between you two went through my heart like a needle.

Of course. I shouldn't have believed you would do something generous with your own motives hiding in the shadows. I pressed my lips into a thin, white line, anger sparking in my chest.

I would not allow you to do this to us. Not again.

"Take a turn with me around the studio, husband," I said, voice light as I rose to my feet. I fixed you with a look that told you I would not accept any refusal, and held my arm out expectantly. You arched an eyebrow but obeyed, winding our arms together as you led me in a slow circle along the edge of the studio. I'm sure our antiquated manners must have looked strange to Gregori, with his radical ideas about equality between the sexes and a society without hierarchy, but I knew my place. I knew the circumstances under which I could request a private word with you, and I knew how to leverage them to the greatest effect.

I waited until we were out of earshot to levy my complaint.

"You want him. The model. I can smell it on you. Like a sickness."

"So do you," you countered. "So does Magdalena. Why should that change anything?"

"Don't make this about me. This is the piece of art you intend for us to take home, is that it? You found a boy. A vulnerable, poor boy and you, what? Picked him out? Made him promises?"

"I did no such thing."

"You're lying," I said through gritted teeth. "God, how many lies have you fed me during our life together? I can scarcely tell them apart from the truth anymore."

"Keep your voice down," you ordered, voice deathly quiet. "You're working yourself into hysterics. Look at me, Constanta my love."

I met your eyes. So very black, like I could fall into them and never find my way out again.

"I haven't deceived you," you said levelly. "Not knowingly, at any rate. Alexi was an accident. But a happy one, don't you think?"

You inclined your head towards the model, who was laughing and flirting with Magdalena. She had drifted towards him and was clutching her purse in her hands as he made her giggle. Her eyes were bright, and there was color in her cheeks. She looked more alive than she had in years, and it was all because of this golden-haired boy with a clever tongue and eyes warm as summer.

"Look how much joy he brings her," you murmured, your mouth as close to my ear as the snake must have been to Eve in the garden. "She's smiling again. When's the last time you saw that?"

"Too long," I admitted miserably.

"Perhaps we could all be that happy," you pressed. "Together."

"He's too young," I said, in one last valiant effort to be the voice of reason. "He's barely more than a child. You would steal the rest of his life from him."

"Look around you. What sort of life is this? When's the last time you suppose he had a good meal? If we leave him he'll starve."

You cupped my face in your hands. Your thumbs made little circles around my cheekbones so tenderly that I almost began to cry. You always knew how to thaw my heart right when I had resolved to freeze it against you.

"We'd be doing him a great kindness, Constanta," you said, your voice soft. "He has no one else."

I should have said no. I should have stamped my foot, or begun to cry, or icily demanded we leave right away. But I didn't. I loved you too much, my lord. I craved you like maidens crave the grave, the way death burns for human touch: inconsolably, unrelentingly, aching for the annihilation in your kiss. I had no practice saying no to you.

And then there was Magdalena, so much like her former self that it brought it tears to my eyes. And this boy, so thin and so beautiful, and so, so young. Alone in a city torn apart by revolution without a mother to make sure he was getting home safe every night. I didn't know how much he made posing for paintings, but it was probably barely enough to buy bread. With us, at least, he would have a chance at happiness.

Or at crushing despair, the same despair that drove you towards frenzied research, that overtook Magdalena in a dark cloud, that drove me weeping into the arms of a God I wasn't sure I still believed in. None of us were immune to it. It was simply a byproduct of our unnatural lives. People aren't meant to live for ever. I know that now.

But then, I was still optimistic. I still wanted to believe I was living in a fairy tale, that I lay down every night with a prince instead of a wolf.

I wanted to believe you.

"I will allow this thing," I whispered. "But for Magdalena's sake, and for the boy's. Not for yours."

It was one of the boldest things I had ever said to you. I expected you to snap at me, but instead you raised your eyebrows and nodded. Almost as if you had stumbled across a newfound respect for me.

"And I'm not saying he can stay for ever," I went on, fingers shaking as I gripped them together behind my back. "I don't need a little brother, or a child to nurse back to health."

Even then, I knew I was lying. I watched him juggle wax apples as Magdalena cheered, the lines of his ribs showing through his thin skin, and I wanted very much to run my fingers through his hair as I held a cup of broth to his lips. I wanted to lay out a feast for him, let him recline on my lap and tell him to eat as much as he wanted.

I had a weakness for weakness, just like you.

"Of course," you said in your voice specifically made

for placating me. The one you made such fragile promises in. "We would have to all agree on something like that."

You swept back over to Alexi, who looked every inch the mythical Ganymede in his drapery. That was probably why he had caught your eye in the first place. You had a dispassionate appreciation for aesthetics; after such a long life only the most perfect symmetries could stop you in your tracks. Still, there was a romantic streak lurking in your rational mind, and you loved to be surrounded by beautiful things while you worked, whether it was the scenic backdrop of an ancient city, the baroque interiors of a fashionable apartment, or the lovely faces of your consorts. You loved to collect and show us off like a tsarina might show off her family jewels.

You carried on a brisk conversation with Alexi while the painter grumbled and tried to capture the curve of Alexi's throat, the inviting divot over his lips. Alexi did his best not to smile or color under your gaze, but he didn't have much success. His eyes kept skittering over to Magdalena and me with a boldness that was almost scandalous. He had no shame, this one.

You caught him looking and gave him a secretive smile. It seemed to give you a particular pleasure, watching him watch us.

"They tell me you have no family to care for you," you said. "Tell me, did you ever wish for sisters?"

Alexi gave a nervous laugh, but I saw a little shudder go through his stomach at your implication. He knew exactly what you were talking about. I wondered how many times you and he had met before. If you had already made him dark promises with your lips on his neck and your hand under his shirt. I shoved this thought down as quickly as I could. You wouldn't do that to us. You had learned your lesson with Magdalena; I was just being paranoid.

"Would you like to leave?" you asked in his ensuing silence. I knew that tone. I had heard it before, in the mud and blood of my home country, and then in Magdalena's palace. It was a quiet double entendre, one question that covered up a much weightier one.

If possible, Alexi colored even more.

"With you?"

"With us."

Magdalena's breath caught next to me, and I felt her heartbeat kick up in the tight grip she had on my hand. I realized that my own breath was fast and shallow. What were we doing? What was I allowing? And why did I feel like I was powerless to stop it?

Alexi swallowed and then nodded, a glazed look in his eyes.

"How much did you pay for him?" you asked the painter, breaking your scorching eye contact with Alexi for only a moment. "What was his sitting fee?"

The painter told you. You produced three times that amount from your purse and pressed it into his hands.

"For robbing you of such an inspiring subject," you said by way of an apology.

You held out a gloved hand to Alexi, welcoming him

through an invisible door that Magdalena and I had already walked through. My heart battered wildly in my chest. Part of me wanted to throw myself between you and Alexi and tell the boy to go home, to forget all he had seen and heard. But another part of me wanted to welcome him into our warm carriage and hand-feed him berries until he was sated.

Alexi let the bolt of fabric slip from his shoulders as he stepped down off his dais. You shrugged off your winter coat of sealskin and draped it around him, and he swayed under the weight of all that finery. Magdalena grinned at this game and stepped forward to claim her prize, removing her mink stole and draping it around his neck. I went last, tugging off my winter gloves as I walked towards the boy whose life I was either about to save or ruin irrevocably.

Alexi's skin was so warm that the tips of my fingers burned when I took his hands in mine. I delicately tugged the fabric over his wrists, feeling the small bones of his hand, so close to the surface. When I met his eyes he was looking at me with absolute reverence, the way a child might look at a statue of the Madonna.

In that moment, a thin fracture ran through my heart that has never been repaired. It was a wound in the shape of Alexi's name, and I scarcely knew how to hold all that feeling inside me. My heart was expanding, making room for him in a world already defined by two great loves, and it hurt so sweetly. But this was different from my obsession with you and my passion for Magdalena. This was the love of the maid for the children in her care, all springtime bloom and tender affection.

It wasn't that I didn't desire him as well. He was breathtaking to look at and the sweet fragrance of his blood ghosted over his skin like baking sugar, making my mouth water. It was just that my will to protect him was that much stronger.

t the time I thought I was protecting him from the world. From war and famine and poverty. But now I know I was also steeling myself to protect him from a much more present threat.

You.

I just wasn't ready to admit that bit to myself yet.

ou led him out the door with your arm possessively around his shoulder, Magdalena and I trailing behind with our arms wound together. The coach waited invitingly, sleek polished walnut gleaming in the winter weather like black blood on new snow.

"Are we going to do it now?" Alexi asked, looking up at you with round eyes. "You said—"

"Discretion," you chided, pulling him closer so no one in the street would overhear. "You promised you were capable of it."

"I am! I just wondered—"

"Yes, we're going to do it now, little prince."

The coach was dim and warm, stuffed with furs and outfitted with a bottle of cold champagne. Alexi settled himself gingerly into his seat like he had never traveled in such accommodations before. His blue eyes gleamed invitingly in the darkness as you helped Magdalena and then myself into the coach by the hand. Finally, you swung yourself inside and ordered the driver to take us all home.

Your mouth was on his the instant the door closed, seeking his kiss like a grieving man seeks strong drink. Alexi shuddered and bloomed under your lips, sliding one arm around your neck while the other reached out for Magdalena. She settled in close beside Alexi, nuzzling at his neck, while I took my seat at your feet. You broke the kiss long enough to turn to me and take my face in your hands, leaving Alexi and Magdalena to each other.

You kissed me deeply, your usually frigid mouth warm with the taste of him, and my muscles slackened beneath your ministrations. Alexi chased Magdalena's kisses with a grin, his white teeth flashing in the confines of the coach. Within moments her hat had been discarded and her hair was falling in ringlets past her shoulders

"I love you," you said into my mouth. It sounded like you were drawing up a peace treaty to protect the boundary lines of contested ground. "I promise you that."

My throat was tight, either with fear or desire or the strange foreboding that had been nipping at my heels since the moment I set eyes on Alexi. I needed fresh air, but the coach was hot and close, and we were already trundling down the road. There was nowhere for me to go. There had never been anywhere for me to go.

"Alexi," you said, voice rough with want. You hauled him onto your lap and took his jaw in your hand. Your grip was just tight enough to leave divots in his skin as the heavy seal coat slipped from his shoulders.

"Are you sure you really want this?" you asked. "You can leave, if you'd like."

Alexi gazed at you, lips reddened with Magdalena's lipstick, his eyes clouded over with an abject devotion so familiar it went through my heart like a dagger. I knew that look. I knew what it felt like to be held by you, suspended in place like a fly trapped in a web. There was no saying no to you, not now, when you had drawn Alexi into your world of lust and finery. He had passed the point of no return the moment you first smiled at him.

I tried very hard not to think of when that might have been. Of how long you had been planning to spirit this boy away.

Alexi wrapped his fingers around your wrist and slid your hand down so it was around his neck, pressing lightly against his jugular.

"This is all I want," he said. "I'm yours."

You looked into his eyes curiously, perhaps wondering if he knew how easy it would be for you to snap his neck. Knowing Alexi, I suspect he did.

"I promise you bread and roe," you declared. "Pheasant and mackerel, vodka and pomegranates from now until eternity. Chairmen and ballerinas will dine at our table and you will know nothing but bounty."

Alexi kissed you again, hungry for his own annihilation. You wound your fingers through my own, drawing me closer, and Magdalena pressed in on your other side, her dark eyes shining with want.

Magdalena bit him first, her sharp teeth pricking his fingertip. He didn't even cry out, just thrust his other hand out to me. How freely he offered himself up! All the enthusiasm of youth with none of the wisdom and caution of age. Hesitation burned in the back of my brain, but the heady scent of blood had started to fill the coach, and Alexi was so lovely and so willing…

I kissed his wrist in an apology before burying my teeth into his skin. His blood was crisp and sweet as a burst grape, dribbling down my chin as I drank from him greedily. I could have drained him dry and still been thirsty for more.

You held him by the throat, watching waves of rapture cross his face while Magdalena and I drank from him. He looked like a lithe young Christ, crucified between two beautiful women with you as his cross.

Alexi gave a little whimper, and for a moment I thought he was begging for the pain to stop. But then I realized he was asking for more.

You tilted his head back and sank your teeth into his jugular, all the way up to the gums. A shudder wracked Alexi's frame.

We three feasted on him for a few delicious minutes before you pulled back, pupils blown with bloodlust and mouth smeared red, and said, "Enough. Enough! He needs to stay conscious. Make room."

Magdalena and I shook off the drunkenness of a freshly opened vein and moved aside so you could lay Alexi down on the seat. His golden skin was alarmingly pale, his breathing shallow and quiet. You gently pulled his head into your lap and I daubed the cold sweat from his forehead with my handkerchief, my fingers seeking his fading pulse. He was dying, and quickly.

Regret, cold and unyielding, settled into my stomach. What had we done?

Alexi moaned something incoherent that sounded close to your name. You shushed him and opened a wound in your wrist with your teeth, staining your white cuffs with blood.

"No need to speak. Just drink."

He parted his lips and you dribbled your own blood, so thick and dark it almost looked black in the low lighting, into his mouth. Alexi took it onto his tongue like a communion wafer and swallowed obediently.

I had attended to Magdalena during her transformation, but that had not felt so much like sitting at someone's deathbed. I truly believe I saw the light wink out of Alexi's eyes before it came back again with renewed brilliance, before he pressed himself up onto his elbows and started lapping at the blood dribbling down your fingertips.

You let out a laugh, all silver and steel, and Magdalena clapped her hands for joy. We were witnessing a rebirth, after all, a dark baptism into a new and unending life. But I could not summon mirth. I had just watched a young boy sign away his life to a pack of demons he barely knew. And now, I believed deeply in my soul, he was my responsibility. I had to protect him from the cruelties of the world, the ravages of immortality. Even from you, my lord.

A lick of anger flamed up in my chest. I had told you not to do this, and here we were again, a growing family despite our incurable dysfunction. But when Alexi's eyes fluttered open and found mine, the anger was smothered by a ferocious tenderness.

"Welcome back, little prince," you said with a smile, smoothing a sweaty curl from his brow. "Where would you like to go?"

"Go?" Alexi asked, a little delirious. It takes a lot out of you, dying and coming back, and I knew the way your blood burned through the system like a wildfire. He was probably so disoriented he was tasting color.

"It's a honeymoon!" Magdalena exclaimed, unable to contain her excitement. I hadn't seen her so effervescent in what felt like years, but this still didn't feel right. Alexi was a boy, not a wind-up doll to cheer up a sullen little girl.

But then again, maybe we would all benefit from some new blood in the family.

Yes, I thought of him as family right away. Even though I told you I wouldn't welcome him into my heart like that. But you've always been able to see through my hopeful lies, haven't you?

"Pick a city," you said. "A country."

"Anywhere?" Alexi asked, accepting my offered handkerchief so he could wipe the blood from his mouth.

"Europe is your playground."

Alexi didn't have to think about it. He just gave a huge, dazzling smile, and I realized with a horrible sense of finality that I was already falling in love with him.

"Paris," he said.

aris was happy, for a time. You rented us a three-story sliver of a townhouse right in the middle of the city, and Magdalena affectionately called it our layer cake. It really did look like one of those delicate French pastries, with a spiked iron gate out front and a wash of pale blue paint over the exterior walls. There was a floor for each of us, not counting the basement, which was set aside for your inscrutable purposes. The longer I spent living with you, the more I came to suspect that you weren't looking for any huge breakthrough or eureka moment. You research had little other purpose than to keep your insatiable curiosity preoccupied so it didn't devour you the moment you turned your back on it. It was a sort of narcissistic love letter to our species, to dedicate so much of your life to exploring the natures of vampires and humans, to draw distinctions between the two.

I tried not to wonder if you had studied your other brides the way you studied us. If you had studied the way they died as well.

Alexi took to the streets of Paris like a fish to water. He would leave for twenty minutes to run an errand and come home bursting with some news of some thrilling performance or political demonstration or literary salon he had been invited to. I have no idea how he managed to make friends so fast, but I was always charmed when he swept Magdalena into his arms and kissed her and started babbling about the newest opera he wanted to sneak her into. You permitted him to accept perhaps one in five of these invitations, but they just kept coming. Paris in the twenties was a living, breathing thing, bursting at the seams with artists and writers and lovers. You and Alexi went out every evening for a walk and a cigarette along the Seine, leaving Magdalena and me two hours of privacy to rest or gossip or tumble into bed.

We took our dinners together every night, with you leading us out on our hunt like a father corralling his unruly brood of children after Sunday mass. Otherwise, you left us to our own devices. You and Magdalena disappeared frequently to hunt for sport, but Alexi and I preferred to do most of our killing privately. I, for my proclivity for stalking my prey into the darkest dens of their sins, and Alexi, for his proclivity to draw his prey into the den of his bedroom first.

I was not invited into his bedroom, at least not at first. That was not the nature of our relationship. We reveled in our love of you, of Magdalena, but the affection between us was more mother and son than lovers. Passion was a boundary line I dared not cross. I wanted Alexi as he was, bright and feckless, and feared jeopardizing the tenderness between us for a few hours of pleasure.

Maybe that's why I tried in vain to protect him, when the fights began.

Alexi got under your skin faster than I or Magdalena ever did, and the spats started shortly after the honeymoon. First it was just irritation, tight in your voice, then the arguments volleyed between the two of you over the tiniest disagreement. Alexi didn't have my knack for making himself invisible when you were in one of your moods, or Magdalena's fawning skill for soothing your temper. He challenged you outright, talking back from the moment he was bitten. He was democratically minded, and he wanted a say in everything, from where we moved to how we spent our days. It reminded me of Magdalena's keen appetite for planning trips in our early days together, or the way I had opened my arms wide to new places and new people when I was young and still flush with life. I didn't realize how resigned Magdalena and I had become to our roles as dutiful wives until Alexi came onto the scene, and his argumentative spirit frightened me. For his sake, mostly.

I did my best to get him out of the house when you were at your most irritable, a reprieve you welcomed. Alexi's energy and appetites were inexhaustible, the enthusiasm of youth captured for ever in an undying body, and he demanded more of your attention than you were willing to give.

"He can be so boorish," Alexi said as we walked arm

in arm through one of Paris's bustling alleyways. Even at night, the city buzzed with life. Cafés spilled light and laughing patrons out onto the street, and the air smelled like coffee and buttered pastries and roasting vegetables. "I don't know how you've managed to put up with him for hundreds of years."

"By trying to stay off his bad side, I suppose," I said, allowing Alexi to lead me around a large puddle in the middle of the street. We must have seemed like an odd pair: Alexi young and handsome in his flashy silk waistcoat and cap cocked at a rakish angle, me in a black dress with a high neck and no adornment to speak of. I had always preferred plain clothes, although your wealth opened up worlds of fine fabrics and expert tailoring to me. They reminded me of the simple dresses I wore as a girl and kept any eyes from lingering on me too long. I liked the invisibility plainness afforded me, unlike Magdalena, who thrived when she was the center of attention.

"Where's the fun in that?" Alexi asked, his laughter bright as a trumpet. He waved at a pretty couple taking wine and cigarettes al fresco in front of a cramped café, and they shouted his name across the street in an attempt to get him to come and sit with them. Another one of his radical friends, I supposed, Nin or Miller or any of their set. Alexi had so many friends their names tended to fall out of my head as soon as he introduced us. I was built for long walks with a single conversation partner, not for Alexi's raucous roundtable discussions. I hoped he wouldn't introduce me.

To my relief, Alexi kept walking, leading me down the street to an antique oddities store that fascinated him. Alexi loved you in part because of your connection with the past. He was always asking for old war stories or tales of your tenure in the palaces of duchesses and kings. He was of the opinion that the past was far more romantic than the present, no matter how voraciously he ate up every bit of sweetness the modern world had to offer. Maybe it was because he had also tasted the cruelties of modernity and lived through so much of its upheaval.

The antique store was dusty and dim, but Alexi's face brightened as soon as we stepped inside as though he had found a doorway to Camelot. He ran his fingers over the pendants and parasols, the cigar boxes and hat boxes, losing himself in the reverie of days gone by. Soon, your morning spat had been entirely forgotten, and he was prattling on about all the historical events he wished he could have lived to see.

I didn't have the heart to tell him that he was sure to live through plenty of history. I doubted he would find it as rarefied an experience as his imagination hoped.

The shopkeeper appeared at the back of the store, a thin man with a nose like a hawk.

"Can I help you find something, young man?"

"We're just taking it all in," Alexi said pleasantly.

"Good. If you or your mother need any help, just ring the bell and I'll be right with you."

He disappeared into the back room, leaving Alexi snickering. I scowled, crossing my arms tight across my chest.

Coming out with Alexi suddenly seemed foolish. That was all anyone ever saw when they looked at us together, a mother and son, or a governess and her overgrown ward. I had a face built for a chaperone, not for making beautiful young men fall in love with me.

"Come now, Constance," Alexi purred soothingly as he sidled up to me. It was his special nickname for me, and it always warmed my heart to hear him say it. "Don't be mad. It's an honest mistake."

"Honest in that I look like a spinster?" I muttered.

Alexi snatched up a nearby silk scarf, fluttering it through the air before looping it around my shoulders. His touch was heavy and warm on my skin, and desire pooled in my stomach. Paris and a steady diet had banished the gaunt look from his features, and I hadn't noticed until that moment how healthy and handsome he had become.

"Honest in that you're motherly," he conceded. "Why, you're a regular Wendy Darling to us lost children."

I couldn't help but smile at the comparison. Alexi had taken me to see the play, and even though I hadn't been a child for a long time, I had a fondness for its charming tale of eternal childhood. Sometimes, rousing Magdalena and Alexi from bed so we could face the night as a family felt like dealing with children.

"Does that make him Peter?" I asked drolly.

"He's certainly moody enough to play the part."

"You haven't seen anything. After that whole debacle with the Harkers he was sullen for months."

"Who are the Harkers?"

"Before your time, dear; just some dreadful Victorians."

Alexi slid the scarf from my shoulders with a theatrical flourish.

"Come on. I'm buying you this, and then we're going for coffee. You can still drink coffee, can you?"

"Yes," I lied. I could manage a few sips, for Alexi.

"Good," he said. "There are people I must introduce you to."

lexi had an appetite for danger. He liked to wear a gun, and to walk along the thin edge of the Seine by night, and to slice shallow cuts into himself to entice Magdalena and me into a frenzied bedroom game. Once, you found us three together: we girls lapping up the blood pooling in Alexi's collarbones like kittens while he made soft, pleasured noises, the bloody pocket knife still in his hands.

You dragged your little finger through the blood on his chest, tracing out the first letter of your name before bringing your finger up to your mouth. To this day, I cannot fathom your restraint. Even the littlest pinprick of blood set me on the hunt, and I was suckling at the cut Alexi had made with an almost painful desire. It took every ounce of self-control I had not to pin him down and tear out his throat, and I'm sure Magdalena felt very much the same. But that, of course, was the sweetness of his game.

"Your thrill-seeking will kill you," was all you said flatly. "You shouldn't drink from each other."

"Why?" Magdalena whined, her mouth smeared with her brother's blood. She didn't get to finish her line of questioning, because I started kissing it off her insistently.

"Because I don't know what the effects are. I haven't done enough research."

"Well then, get in here and do some research," Alexi said, pulling you into bed.

His charms were hard to resist, as you well knew, and so did half the city of Paris. Alexi must have had a hundred friends scattered throughout the city, and he did his best to split this time between all of them. You disapproved of these connections and did your best to keep him at home, within arm's reach. Relationships with humans were all doomed from the start, you insisted. Either they died unexpectedly, breaking your heart, or they caught on to your true nature eventually and had to be put down. But Alexi wouldn't be deterred. He kept befriending actors and poets and jazz musicians, and he kept pushing you to let him roam freely outside the house.

"It's been ages since I was on the stage," Alexi pleaded one night. We were all coming back from a night at the theatre, taking our time walking home in the warm summer air. "Why won't you let me audition?"

"Because it's dangerous," you said with a heavy sigh. This was not the first time you and Alexi had had this conversation. "Eventually, people would start asking questions. They would notice that you don't age. Use your head, Alexi."

"Then I'll switch troupes! You've never even seen me

act; I was very good! I would be responsible, I promise."

You gave him an indulgent smile.

"Why don't you do a monologue for us at home, then? We can have our own private performance; we don't need all those other people. Besides, I don't want to share you with them."

You were speaking in a low, cajoling voice, the way you spoke to him when you were trying to entice him into your bed. Alexi didn't look convinced, but he nodded anyway.

Later that night, Magdalena accentuated his features with dabs of her makeup while I created a backdrop of bedsheets. He performed scene after scene from memory, declaring valiant love before launching into a tyrant's tirade and then dying beautifully on the ground as Romeo. You cheered him on and tucked roses into his lapel, waxing poetic about his once-in-a-century talent. Alexi, ever a lover of the spotlight, grinned so wide that I thought his face might get stuck that way.

"See?" you said. "You don't need to go running around on stage with the rabble of Paris. Our home will be your theatre, and we your devoted audience."

Alexi's smile faltered a little, but he let you kiss him all the same.

Alexi was entirely rapt by you, following you around like a dog at the heels of its master. He adored everything about you, good and bad, from your soft-spoken declarations of love to your flashes of foul temper. The love he had for you was the cartographer's love for the sea, trembling and all-consuming and so far beyond the reaches of right or wrong. Far from shrinking from your bad moods, he welcomed them.

Alexi provoked and riled you at every turn, seeming to delight in the conflict, and he did whatever he pleased despite your litany of rules. Nothing was sacred to Alexi, and he was happy to commit the most outlandish and egregious of faux pas whenever it pleased him. For the most part, you ignored his antics as though he were a misbehaving child, probably hoping he would settle into his new life with time. But the opposite happened. The longer Alexi lived with us, the more restless he became. Eventually, even your sweetest words and most luxurious gifts couldn't placate him.

One night, you and I came back from the hunt to find all the lights burning in the apartment. We were greeted at the door by the sounds of tinkling champagne glasses and uproarious laughter, sounds so foreign to that house.

You froze in the entryway, your hand still gripping the door knob, and listened in gobsmacked silence for a moment.

"Alexi," you growled.

I followed after you at a brisk clip as you strode down the hallway towards the parlor. Alexi lounged on the couch with a glass of wine in his hand, holding court over a ragtag group of seven or eight actors. I assumed they were actors from their florid but frayed clothes, and the smears of greasepaint still clinging to hairlines and shirt cuffs.

Far from looking contrite, Alexi burst into a smile when he saw you.

"Darling!" he crowed, beckoning you over. "Come have a drink with us."

You stood glowering in your own parlor, looking like the Red Death come to break up a lively party. There was no way you would have given Alexi your approval to bring people over to the house. It was our sanctum; no one stepped foot inside except servants and meals.

You deliberately removed your gloves one finger at a time.

"Alexi," you repeated, heavy and low. You had an uncanny ability to turn any of our names into a warning when you wanted to.

Alexi ignored the threat, slinging his arm around the shoulders of a young man seated next to him on the sofa. The boy was gangly and hadn't quite grown into his limbs yet, around the same age Alexi had been when you turned him. Magdalena sat on his other side, looking entirely enchanted by the ruckus in her living room. She had probably been surprised when he brought the actors home, but she didn't seem upset at the diversion in the slightest.

"These fine players just closed a marvelous show," Alexi prattled on. "Totally modern, *avant garde*, as they say. It was a revelation. Come, sit with us! Constance, you too, dear one."

I looked to you for my cue but you were staring straight ahead at Alexi, boring holes into him with your eyes. Eventually, you gave a dismissive wave of your hand, bidding me sit. You stalked over to an open armchair and perched yourself on the edge of it, your face dangerously placid. I never knew what was going on beneath the surface when you arranged your features like that. It frightened me.

"Magdalena, what's going on?" I whispered to her sidelong.

She colored a bit.

"I know I should have turned them away, but it was just so nice to have company after all this time . . . Alexi said he had permission."

"Alexi is a liar," I muttered back, looking between our golden prince's smiling face and your stony one. He had bitten off more than he could chew this time, I was sure of it. There was going to be hell to pay the instant you two were alone together.

But I could hardly blame Alexi for bringing the merry band home, or blame Magdalena for letting them in. They filled the living room with light and sound, and made the drafty old apartment seem snug and lived-in. A party was just what these beautiful old rooms needed, I decided. That was how they were meant to be appreciated.

A pretty young woman in a shift dress and feather earrings circled the room, pouring the dregs of a wine bottle into mismatched glasses. They had raided our untouched kitchen and made free with what they found there, apparently. I smiled weakly at her when she pressed a glass into my hand. Then she moved on to you, suddenly looking a little nervous under the weight of your eyes.

"Do you drink wine?" she asked hesitantly. "We've got absinthe, too."

You smiled at her, cloying and irresistible. A little shudder went through her and she gave a laugh. The next thing I knew you had gallantly taken her by the hand and pulled her into your lap.

Warm laughter rippled through the room, and Alexi clapped his hands in approval. His pretty friend flushed and covered her mouth with her hand, but her eyes sparkled with delight. Who could deny you, after all, with that rakish smirk on your face?

I clutched my glass of wine warily, marveling at your sudden good humor. It wasn't unheard of for your mood to change on a dime. But it usually swept from content to contemptuous, not the other way around.

"You see?" Magdalena whispered to me with a smile. "It will all be all right."

You kissed the girl's wrist and murmured something to her. She leaned in closer to hear you over the happy chatter of the party, her chestnut curls falling to the side to expose a beautiful brown throat. You lightly kissed the juncture of her neck and shoulder, earning a flutter of her dark lashes.

Then you parted your lips against her skin, gently at first, until I could see the sheen of your teeth all the way across the room.

"Don't—" I started, pushing myself to my feet.

You squeezed her hand and drove your teeth into her neck, holding her fast when she screamed and tried to wrench away.

The room erupted into chaos. Alexi's friends shrieked and dropped their glasses onto the rug; they shot to their feet and clutched each other in terror. It all happened so fast, none of us had any time to so much as formulate a sentence.

You dropped the girl's body unceremoniously to the ground. It slumped onto the hardwood, glassy-eyed and pale.

Alexi screamed your name. I barely heard him over the clatter and rush of bodies fleeing the room. In moments, all of his friends were gone.

Magdalena shrieked her rage. She was on her feet, fists trembling at her sides. I was frozen, my wine glass shattered at my feet while I watched the life drain out of that poor girl's eyes.

"What have you done!" Magdalena wailed.

"Go to your room, Magdalena," you snapped, wiping the blood from your mouth with the cuff of your shirt. "I don't want to look at you. This is your doing, you and Alexi."

"How can you possibly say—?"

"*Leave us*," you hissed.

Magdalena opened her mouth to argue with you, but the ferocity of your gaze silenced her. She stalked out of the room, slamming the door behind her hard enough that I jumped. I was still rooted to the couch, struck with shock.

Alexi was having fits. He hadn't stopped screaming at you since you bit that girl, and now, in the ensuing quiet of the near-empty living room, I could finally make out what he was saying.

"You bastard! You absolute monster!"

"We *are* monsters, Alexi," you shot back, thrusting your hand towards the dead body. "This is what comes from forgetting that. How could you be so careless and stupid to bring humans into this house? This is what happens to them, you know that."

"They're my friends!" Alexi shouted, going red in the face. He looked every inch the petulant prince in his loose white shirt, but his rage was that of a grown man. "Why don't you let any of us have friends?"

In any other scenario you would have walked out and left Alexi with his tempestuous emotions, but he was blocking your way to the door. I knew from experience that if Alexi kept pushing you, you would explode. I tensed involuntarily.

"They aren't friends. They're humans. Prey animals, ghosts of a past life. You forget yourself, Alexi."

"I'm not forgetting anything! Sometimes I feel like I'm the only one around here who remembers anything. The taste of food, the feel of warm skin, the sound of laughter."

"Alexi," I said quietly, holding my arms out to him.

"Don't defend him!" Alexi shouted. "All you ever do is defend him."

His words pricked my heart like a hornet sting, but I knew he was right. All those years living under your thumb and I still justified your behavior to the others, hoping to make sense of the madness.

"Alexi," you hissed.

He turned the full force of his wrath back onto you. "I didn't sign up to waste away in some tower room while the world went on turning outside. You told me I would live. I want to *live*."

"The world has no place for us," you snapped, eyes flashing dark fire. "We are wanderers by nature, lions among lambs. We have no recourse to our food."

"Just shut up and listen to me," Alexi shouted, tears springing to his eyes. I had seen Alexi cry only a handful of times in our years together, and the sight frightened me. I wanted terribly to fold him up in my arms and hide him away from you, but this was his fight. He had been itching for it for months, and I wasn't going to rob him of it. "I need friends. Don't you understand? The way I need blood, or rest. I'll lose my mind without them."

"You have your sisters."

"We cannot exist only for each other!" Alexi screamed, right in your face.

You slapped him.

It was a sharp, deliberate slap, and the force nearly knocked Alexi to the ground.

hat slap snapped me out a reverie I had been living in for hundreds of years. It obliterated any grace I had left to give you, any lies I was still telling myself about your good intentions and your savior's heart.

I had always comforted myself in the dark hours after any of our arguments with the thought that at least you had never hurt any of us. You would *never* hurt any of us. You only wanted what was best for us, and you were harsh with us because you loved us.

But now, all my carefully crafted excuses for you dissolved like sugar under absinthe, revealing a truth I had spent centuries avoiding.

You hit him," I blurted. It was the only thought screaming through my mind. "Oh my God. You hit him."

"We're leaving," you announced, looking a little unsteady, as though you were surprised by your own violence. You always prided yourself on your restraint, after all. "Pack your things. Both of you."

I rushed over to Alexi and pulled him into my arms, letting him bury his face in my bosom.

"You can't just make us leave," Alexi spat, cradling his wounded cheek in his hand. The fight hadn't gone out of him entirely, but the fire of his rage had been dampened. "We have a life here."

"Any life you had here died with her," you said, jutting your chin towards the corpse quickly going cold on the rug. "There were witnesses, Alexi. A half-dozen of them. They know what you are now, and they'll run you through with a hot iron or make you eat silver bullets if they see you again. The police will be coming soon, looking for death and someone to blame. Do you really want to be here when they arrive?"

"Do not do this," I heard myself say. I felt so small, so pathetic and useless. You had exposed us to the world through an act of senseless violence. Even worse, you had laid hands on my beloved Alexi right in front of me and here I was, pleading like a schoolgirl. I should have torn your throat out in that very instant, and every day I regret that I was too frightened to try. "Don't drag us out onto the road again."

You gave me an almost pitying look. It made me sick to my stomach.

"None of you have left me any choice," you said.

he château you found for us was miles away from the nearest city, a crumbling pastoral house that had seen better days. The money had begun to run out by then, I suspect. No amount of sound investments and jewels handed down through generations could outlive the slow grind of time, and our lifestyles had become less and less extravagant in recent years. Our finances were in as much a state of decay as that house was, wasting away with stubborn slowness.

You shut us up in that great house like misbehaving children in a nursery. Every door was locked and every shutter was closed, ensconcing us in a world of eternal night. You added locks to all the windows and doors, claiming that they were to keep out the superstitious peasants, but they locked from the outside and you carried the key around with you at all times.

Magdalena lapsed into melancholy and took to spending long intervals in her room alone, languishing under silk sheets and refusing food for days at a time. I wandered the halls during the days, sleepless as a mad woman from a Gothic novel. Alexi, for his part, railed. He became prone to fits of rage that reminded me so much of you that my chest hurt, bursting into shouts or slamming his hands against the locked door at the slightest provocation. It was never directed at us girls, always at you, at his circumstances, but I still ached for him. I wanted to spirit him away from your corrosive influence, nurse his heart back to health somewhere where the doors were always open and no one ever raised their voices except in mirth.

As the days wore on, my hopes seemed more like flights of fancy. We were entirely alone, out in the country without any reprieve from your tyrannical chaperonage, and the villagers around us were suspicious gossips. None of them would help us, I was sure. They would sooner bind us hand and foot and offer us up to the parish priest as devils in need of exorcisms. Word traveled fast in small villages, and it was common knowledge that the strange disappearances of unattended maidens had only happened after we moved in.

I chafed against the rustic meals, all the more sick with the knowledge that I was dining on innocents. They were peasant girls, just as I had been a peasant girl once, open-hearted and trusting. You strictly forbade me from any of my avenging tendencies and did all the hunting for us, leaving us alone in the house for long stretches of time. I wondered if withholding yourself for those hours was another kind of punishment. You would think we would be happy to be rid of you, but we had been weaned on you like children on mother's milk, and we were always just as relieved to see you come home as we were to see you ride off. You had debased us all over time, as slow as dripping water wearing a hole in stone. We couldn't abide you, but we couldn't live without you.

"He's like a sickness," Alexi said, lying close beside me on Magdalena's lace-trimmed bed. She was having one of her good days, when she was awake for most of the night and bright-eyed.

"How so?" I asked, my fingers latticed over my belly.

"Being around him is like burning up with fever. I know I'm not well, but I'm too delirious to do anything. What medicine is there for that sort of thing?"

"A bracing walk through the cold," Magdalena murmured. "And patience. Fevers have to burn themselves out."

"But he won't," Alexi said, his voice a hoarse whisper. I didn't know if he was furious or on the brink of tears. Both, probably. "He just goes on burning. And I can't look away."

"Tell him so yourself," I ventured, even though I knew that none of us were so brave. "Maybe he'll take it in his stride."

Alexi gave me a withering glance. "After you, dear sister. What did you call him last week? A despot? I'm sure he'd love to hear that."

I lay there in silence for a long while, turning the treacherous beginnings of a plan over in my mind. It was only an inkling of a thing then, hazy and indistinct. But for the first time in a long time, I supposed that there was something to be done about our situation. About you.

I tucked the idea away in a dark recess of my mind and let it ferment.

lexi fell back on old habits and took to stealing. He would secret tiny baubles or bits of silverware in his pockets, hiding it away in his room for some uncertain future. I pretended not to see him, of course. I supposed I shouldn't besmirch him whatever simple outlet for rebellion he had, especially since you kept him on such a tight leash in those days. You trotted him out to perform for us every fortnight, encouraging him to learn new monologues and scenes to entertain with. I suspect you hoped to keep his mind diverted and his hands busy, but he resented the lack of a true audience, the loss of the camaraderie of a band of players.

When he complained, you plied him with kisses or wine, or shouted at him so ferociously the rafters shook. You even seemed jealous when he took refuge with us girls, locking himself away in Magdalena's room to cry into her silk pillowcases and demand that I do something, anything to fix your beastly behavior. You were content to share Alexi with us so long as he remained soundly in your thrall. When he started to wander out of your grasp, you tightened your grip so much he could scarcely breathe.

Once, I passed the cracked door to your room and overheard your voice, sharp with irritation.

"What's the meaning of this?" you asked. "Alexi, look at me when I'm talking to you."

Overcome with curiosity, and a little worried for Alexi's sake, I slipped towards the door and peered cautiously through the crack. If things got too heated between the two of you, God forbid violent, I could make up some excuse to spirit Alexi away.

Alexi was standing in front of you with his head bowed, kicking at the tassel on the rug like a schoolboy. You loomed over him, one of your silver pocket watches dangling from your hands.

"I found this under your pillow," you went on. "Really? Stealing? After all I've done for you, after all I've given to you. Why?"

Alexi muttered something indecipherable, and you tossed your head like an agitated stallion.

"You don't know? Really, you don't know? Try *harder*, Alexi."

There was a threat in your voice he seemed to pick up, because Alexi lifted his head and spoke up.

"I wanted to have something to pawn. Just in case. You've been so bored of me recently, I can tell. I annoy you, and you find me childish, and you'd rather it just be the girls and you. You're going to turn me out soon, I just know it."

You stared at him for a moment, gobsmacked. Then you set the pocketwatch down on the table and massaged your brow with a weary hand.

"Alexi, Alexi," you said, sounding ancient. You took his face between your hands, tall and dark as a specter as you ran your thumbs over his plump cheeks. "I will never get rid of you, do you understand? I sired you and you are mine. Neither hell nor high water nor any machination of man nor beast can change that."

Alexi huffed, but his eyes softened a little.

"Really?"

"Yes. And if we should ever be parted, my prince, I would hunt you down across the continents like my own little rabbit, do you understand?"

"Yes," Alexi said quietly.

"Good," you replied, kissing him sweetly and tugging him towards your bed. "No more stealing, understood? If you want something, just ask for it. Now come here."

"But Maggie and I were going to play cards, I—"

"Hush," you urged, pushing him down onto the rich fabric. "You talk too much."

You knelt between his legs as your deft fingers found the lacing on his pants. Alexi knotted his brow and opened his mouth as though he had more to say but then, perhaps heeding your words, he simply threaded his fingers through your dark hair.

Alexi gasped when you took him expertly into your

mouth, throwing his eyes around the room. In one shocking instant, they fell on me, still poised in the open sliver of the doorway in case I needed to intervene.

I flushed as deeply as my undead state would allow, then gathered my skirts in my hands and rushed away down the hallway.

I found Alexi crying once, pressed into a darkened alcove of the wallpapered hallway. He was scrubbing at his red eyes with the heel of his hand, his blond curls disheveled as though he had been raking his fingers through them.

"Alexi?" I whispered, holding the flame of my candle up close to his face.

He recoiled, wrenching his face away from the flame like it was sunlight and burying himself deeper into the dark corner. I reached out a hand and touched his shoulder, felt the firm muscle beneath his shirt.

"What's happened, Alexi? You can be frank with me. You know you can."

He looked up at me with such a miserable, bitter expression I barely recognized him. Then he crossed his arms and let out a huff, every inch the petulant child.

"What do you think happened to me?"

The air left my lungs in a deflated rush. Of course. Who else in this house could bring somebody to tears like that?

I set the candle down on an end table and eased my arms around his neck, pulled him into a tight hug. I smoothed his hair back from his forehead and he clung to me as tightly as death, his shoulders shaking as the last of the sobs wracked his body.

"Do you think he knows?" he whispered, face buried in my hair. His breath was hot on my neck. "He must not know how *cruel* he can be, how he cuts right to the heart of you, otherwise he wouldn't . . . No one who *knew* would keep doing it over and over again, would they?"

"Oh, Alexi," I breathed. I drew away from him by a few inches, cradling his face in my hands. I gently rubbed the crease from between his brows with my thumb, then began kissing the tears from his cheeks.

"Alexi, Alexi," I repeated like a mantra. He gripped my arms and pulled me closer, turning his face into my kisses. One moment I was kissing his cheekbone, the dimple a few inches below, and then his mouth was on mine, warm and insistent and real. Heat flooded my chest in a rush as I kissed him back. I hadn't felt this alive in a hundred years, I realized. Lately, I hadn't been feeling alive at all.

I let Alexi press me back against the alcove and we disappeared into the sweet, forgiving darkness. His hands roamed down my waist and under my dress, hiking the skirts high. I devoured him with kisses, chasing his mouth whenever he drew away for a single instant. I had never allowed myself to want this because I assumed it wasn't a possibility. I had assumed he was too enthralled by your charms and Magdalena's sunny smiles to even notice me in this way. But now, with Alexi's hand cupping my bottom and his stubble scraping my cheek, I realized how long I had been concealing a treacherous hope.

Our lovemaking was hurried and amateurish and all the sweeter for it, Alexi pressing inside me while I twined my fingers in his hair and urged him on with soft repetitions of his name. We gasped and clung to each other in the alcove, kissing each other as though those would be our last kisses ever on the earth. I came quickly and with a cry, my hips braced securely against the wall while Alexi took me under my dress.

When he finished, he sagged against me, the curls at the nape of his neck tight with sweat. It was such a small, human detail that I suddenly wanted to cry. Young. Alexi was so young. What had we done to him, bringing him into this life?

"Little Alexi," I murmured as he nuzzled my throat.

"I love you, Constance."

Somehow, it sounded like an apology, and the tears pricking my eyes threatened to spill over.

"I know, my darling."

We were both a mess, but managed to right our clothes and smooth each other's hair into some semblance of order. I pressed a kiss to the palm of his hand and released him into the heart of the house, praying that he found his way to refuge before the monster roaming the halls caught him by the scruff of the neck and dragged him back into an argument.

I met the monster myself minutes later in the hallway, when I almost collided with you as you stalked around a corner.

"Have you seen Alexi?" you demanded, not even looking at me. "He's being hysterical."

"Oh, I . . . That is to say, I haven't, ah . . ."

Your eyes flashed over to me as you opened your mouth to snap, but I must have been very obvious, with high color in my cheeks and my dress askew. Or maybe your keenly developed predator senses could smell him on me.

"Oh," you said, voice thick with disdain. "He was with you."

"My lord," I began breathlessly. "I didn't intend—"

You pressed past me as you continued on your mission, barely pausing long enough to throw me a flat final word.

"He only fucked you because he was angry with me and Magdalena's been sick for three days. You know that, don't you?"

Yes, I decided as I gasped for breath, run through with the rapier of your words even as you disappeared down the hallway. *He knows how cruel he can be.*

here was no huge argument that predicated my decision to betray you, no ultimate act of tyranny. I simply broke under the weight of a thousand tense nights, a thousand thoughtless, soul-stripping words. I felt like I was losing my mind in that place, and eventually my desire to do something about it, anything about it, outweighed my fear of you.

e had lived in the house for months, maybe years, before I had the courage to act. I immediately implicated Magdalena and Alexi. I had spent so long trying to protect them from you, but there was no way forward without their help.

"Are you out of your mind?" Magdalena whispered. She had taken to lowering her voice, even when you weren't around to overhear her. At the moment, you were out hunting. We had a scarce hour or two to ourselves before you came back.

"Aren't you at least a little curious?" I pressed. The three of us were huddled around a flickering candelabra in one of the many parlors. The house was not outfitted for electricity, and so we made do with firelight. "About what we might learn?"

"What you're proposing is suicide," Magdalena went on. "What if he catches you in there, rooting around in his things? God, I don't even want to think about it."

"He won't catch her," Alexi chimed in. "He's miles

away tempting some milksop out of the village so we can all eat. We've got a little time."

"What exactly are you hoping to find?" Magdalena asked.

I fixed my mouth into a grim line.

"Anything that will get us out of this place. This is no life. You can't tell me that you're happy here, like this."

"Of course not," she muttered. "But I'd just as soon walk into the sun as I would go rooting around in his things, looking for answers to questions he won't let us ask."

"He knows more than we do," I said, voice pleading. "We don't even know the full range of our power because he's kept it from us."

"He wants to keep up docile and complacent," Alexi said. "Like pets. Don't you want to know how we came to be?"

"Or how ones like us might be killed," I added quietly.

Both Magdalena and Alexi looked at me with shock.

"You can't mean . . ." Alexi began.

"Sister, be *reasonable*," Magdalena finished.

I pulled them both into a tight hug, my heart hammering in my chest. We stood like that for a moment, the three of us entwined and shadowed by the flickering candles, until I began to speak.

"I should have told you both a long time ago, but I was afraid. Of losing him. Losing you both. But I've done this once before. And I'm terrified by what I found."

I told them. I told them what I had discovered and what you had implied; that there had been brides before, a countless number, and none of them had outlived loving you. I spared no detail, and soon Alexi was trembling beneath my touch.

"We're all in danger," I whispered. "If he grows too displeased with us, if we no longer entertain him . . ."

Magdalena had turned to steel in my arms. She held me tight as death, thinking for a long while.

"We're disposable to him," she said finally. Her voice was stiff. "Replaceable."

"I'm sorry," I whispered. "I should have said more, I should have done something before now. But I was so afraid of him."

"Don't you dare apologize," Magdalena said, dark eyes flashing with passion. "I never want to hear you apologize for something he's done ever again. It has to stop, Constanta. It all has to stop."

"What are we going to do?" Alexi asked quietly. He looked very pale and very, very young.

"Uncover what he keeps hidden from us," I said. "Alexi, you can pick locks, can't you?"

"That's right," he said, still looking a little dazed. Finding out your husband would kill you at the drop of a hat was destabilizing, I knew that well. "I used to spring locks all the time when I was squatting with my friends. It's easy enough."

"I'll need you to come with me as far as the door, then. You don't have to come inside if you don't want to."

"I'm not afraid of him," he said, puffing out his chest. A bold-faced lie, but a valiant one. "And I'm not letting you go by yourself. Maggie?"

Magdalena was gazing off into the distance with a hard stare, her lips pressed into a thin line. She was probably thinking of all the ways she wanted to punish you for your duplicitousness.

"Someone has to stay on the ground floor to welcome our dear husband home," she said slowly. "Just in case he arrives while you two are still otherwise occupied."

Alexi sucked in a breath through his teeth.

"If you cover for us and we're found out, you'll be paying double hell. You know he hates it when we take each other's side."

"He won't find out," she said, squeezing his shoulder reassuringly. "Because I'm more clever than him by half."

"So we're agreed?" I asked.

Your voice, sneering and snide, came into my mind. Levelling all sorts of ugly words at me. *Ungrateful. Unfaithful. Mutinous.*

I smothered the thoughts with a quick litany, begging any saint who would still listen to give me strength.

Alexi gave a decisive nod.

"Absolutely."

"Then we'd better get going. He could be back any minute."

I seized Alexi's hand and we started to bustle out of the room, but Magdalena's voice stopped me at the door.

"Constanta?"

"Yes?" I asked, turning back around.

Her eyes were as dark as a night without stars.

"Find out how to make him hurt."

he basement was vast and dark, running almost the entire length of the house. Alexi made short work of the lock on the door with one of my hairpins, and then we carefully traversed the stairs one after the other. I could hear Alexi breathing behind me, shallow, quick breaths betraying his fear. He was terrified of being caught down here, but he had come with me anyway, and I was deeply grateful for his bravery.

The floor of the basement was made of damp earth tightly packed by thousands of footsteps. We picked our way through moldering wooden chests and shelves of wine left to age, doing our best to navigate without bumping into anything. My eyesight was keen in the dark, but Alexi was too young to have developed the skill yet. He followed closely, one hand clutching the sleeve of my dress so we wouldn't be separated.

It didn't take long to find your hideaway. I could make out the shape of two long tables littered with ephemera, and after some groping around, I found an old oil lamp.

Alexi, who was clever enough to always carry a pocket-knife and matches, lit the lamp and cast its glow on the room.

Your strange devices looked even more ghoulish in the flickering firelight. Forceps and vials, eclectic light bulbs and compasses, all scattered around in an arrangement that only made sense to you.

One of the tables had been cleared into a makeshift gurney, and the wood was stained with blood. Perhaps you had carried out one of your experiments on a victim after you had drained them. Or before.

Alexi held the lamp high and we set about trying to find something, anything in the mountains of research to arm us against you. We rifled through books heaped upon books, case study notes, and scientific journal articles, none of which contained what we were looking for. It didn't help that we had to painstakingly return the papers exactly the way we had found them, which caused us to hemorrhage time. With each passing minute, my dread steadily grew. How long had we been down here? Ten minutes? Twenty? We could have spent the whole day down there and still not found what we were looking for, but we didn't have that kind of time.

In the end, it was only sheer, blind luck that saved us. Alexi was flipping through a heavy leather-bound journal he had found stacked up with other books, and he gasped out loud.

"Constance! Come look at this."

I pressed in close to him so we could share the light

of the lamp, and flipped lightly through the journal. It was full of your looping, tight hand, pages upon pages of your personal theories and thoughts. It was not a diary. It was a casebook, containing all you knew about the nature of vampires.

"This is it," I whispered.

I flipped faster through the pages, digesting everything I could. You had laid out your theories about our bodily processes, our strange hungers, our heightened abilities that came with age. You had also documented how long a vampire might be expected to live, if no act of brutality got in their way. You had jotted down a few quick notes about one death you had personally carried out. Your sire, I realized. The man whose blood had made you strong enough to sire vampires of your own.

My breath was as quick and shallow as Alexi's now, my pulse roaring in my ears. He must have sensed that I had struck upon something, because he pushed in tighter to me.

"What is it?"

My fingers trailed down the page, committing every word to memory.

"Freedom," I said.

Alexi never got the chance to ask me what I meant, because somewhere distantly in the house, a door opened and slammed shut. I heard the lilt of Magdalena speaking, her words indistinguishable, and then, unmistakably, the baritone of your voice.

I slammed the book shut and shoved it back in its

place. Alexi was already scrambling back for the stairs, hauling me behind him with a tight grip on my wrist.

"We're dead," he huffed, more to himself than me. "If he finds us down here . . ."

"He won't," I whispered, feigning surety. "Hurry, little Alexi."

We doused the lamp and hustled up the stairs as quietly as we could, pausing for only a moment at the landing to catch our breath and lock the door.

Magdalena had detained you in the foyer and was chattering on prettily about something that was just barely holding your interest. You threw your eyes around the room, shrugging off your coat.

"Where are your siblings?" you asked.

"Here we are," I said, keeping my voice even, my expression pleasant.

I realized how it must have looked, Alexi and I both emerging shamefaced and out of breath, lingering close to one another. Sometimes you were jealous when you had to share us with one another and sometimes you weren't; it was impossible to predict. But you had taken Alexi finding refuge in my arms particularly badly, your dark mood clouding our household for weeks after you found me in the alcove. Probably because you knew it was you he was seeking refuge from.

"Did you bring me something to eat?" Alexi asked in a breezy affect that didn't quite fit the situation. He hadn't sized you up quick enough to realize that you had gotten home irritated and that your mood was only worsening.

"I wasn't able to," you said, voice clipped as you threw your gloves onto a nearby ottoman.

"What do you mean?"

"I was seen," you said, your brows drawn tight together in consternation. "I had to abandon the hunt before it was finished."

"Seen?" Magdalena echoed, crossing her arms over her chest. She raised a disapproving eyebrow at you, and you bristled dangerously.

"Yes, need I repeat myself?"

"The villagers are going to come looking for you, then. They'll bring guns. Weapons even you can't outrun."

You dismissed her fears with a wave of your hand.

"They won't. They're too scared."

Magdalena let out a short, cruel laugh, and I could see the flash of rage beneath. She had been able to hold back her contempt for you and your secrets while distracting you, but now the mask was slipping.

"They're going to topple your little regime," she went on. "All because you were spied nibbling on some stable hand in an alley, is that it?"

Your temper snapped. You took a threatening step forward, and I threw myself between your bodies before I had the chance to think it through.

"Don't touch her," I hissed with more force than I would have thought possible just days before. But, like Eve, I had taken a bite of forbidden fruit and been rewarded with all the knowledge I had hitherto been denied. I knew just as much as you, and I knew you were just as mortal as any human man, under the right circumstances. You could kill us, yes. But that meant you could also be killed.

You staggered back as though I had spat at you, confusion flashing across your face. Then your eyes darkened and before I had the chance to run, you seized me by the throat.

I let out a horrible, ugly gasp, and I saw Alexi move in a blur at my side. Moving to strike you, but Magdalena held him back.

"I'm getting tired of you constantly undermining me," you said through grit teeth.

I writhed under your punishing grip, tears springing to my eyes. You squeezed so hard I saw stars.

"I won't tolerate sedition," you said, bringing your face close to mine. "I made you and I can unmake you. You belong to me, Constanta. Blood of my blood, flesh of my flesh. Say it."

"Blood of your blood," I wheezed, barely able to form the words.

You tossed me aside and I let out a cry like a kicked dog when I hit the floor.

You had a few choice words for Magdalena and Alexi, but I didn't hear them. I was crumpled on the ground, massaging my throbbing neck as sobs wracked my body. I was shaking like a leaf in the wind, more terrified of you than I had ever felt.

As soon as you had stalked down the hallway, Alexi and Magdalena were at my side, cooing gently and petting my hair.

I brought shaking fingers away from my bruised throat, and Magdalena dropped the lightest of healing kisses on the wounded spot.

"Did you find anything?" she whispered into my hair.

I nodded and swallowed hard. I had found something else too, buried deep underneath habit and fear and years of loyalty to you. Anger, white-hot and blinding. Bright enough to illuminate even the darkest night.

"Yes. I found what I was looking for."

Magdalena cast a wary glance over to Alexi and then back to me.

"We three are in agreement, then. We will stand against him?" Magdalena said.

Alexi squared his shoulders and in that moment he looked every inch a prince, ready to lead his troops into war.

"We don't have any other choice."

he villagers arrived before we could fully formulate our plan. It only took them a few days to gather their courage and assemble a small band of men, armed with axes and guns. They crested over the hills shortly after nightfall, marching with lanterns held high and murder in their eyes.

Alexi saw them first, and burst into your room to beg you to do something about it. One or two humans were no problem for creatures such as us, but there were at least two dozen men out there, armed to the teeth. Ready to draw blood after finding you curved over the body of a boy, draining him of life. Provincial life had preserved old superstitions, and I suspect they knew exactly what you were. They had come to root out the preternatural scourge in their midst, who surely must be responsible for the rash of disappearances that had been afflicting the nearby towns.

We had tried to warn you about hunting from so small a pool. It was bound to attract the wrong kind of attention. But keeping us isolated was more important to you than keeping us all safe.

"Let them come," you said, turning your nose up at Alexi's terror. "You think I haven't seen my fair share of mobs before? They won't get past the front gates. They'll sooner piss themselves with fear."

"They're angry," Magdalena said, peering out the window with her hand pressed to her chest. "And they're grieving. Do not underestimate what they're capable of."

"Shouldn't we be running?" Alexi asked, his voice tight. "Or building a barricade?"

"All the doors and windows are locked," you said, a fact we all knew intimately well. You stood in the window, filling the frame with your glowering presence as you watched them approach the front gate. "The house is a labyrinth, with no electric light. If they're stupid enough to wander in we'll pick them off one by one."

Magdalena made a concerned noise but said nothing.

"I'll go push some furniture in front of the door," I said warily, pushing myself up out of my seat. I cast a surreptitious glance to Alexi and Magdalena, who scurried out behind me. Perhaps, on any other day, you would have detected the hint of a coup in the air. But that day, you were too wrapped up in your own arrogance and you own anger to realize something was amiss inside the house, and that was to be your undoing.

"We should do it now," I whispered, tugging my two loves down the corridor with me. "We're running out of time."

Magdalena's eyes were clouded over with thought. This was not like her, to strike in the spur of the moment. She favored careful, quiet planning, like a spider who spun a web for days on end simply to attract the perfect fly.

"We don't have much of a choice," I pled. "He's distracted. We may never get this chance again."

Alexi looked between the two of us, chewing on his lip. He always did that when he was nervous.

"But, Constance . . . He does love us, in his way. It seems wrong to . . ." Alexi swallowed hard, shaking his head. "He loves us. I know it."

This snapped Magdalena out of her reverie. She clasped Alexi by the shoulders and fixed him with a hard, knowing look that I have never forgotten, not even after all these years.

"It would be easier if he hated us," she said. "But he loves us all terribly. And if we go on letting him love us, that love is going to kill us. That's what makes him so dangerous."

Every word felt like a stone pressing down on my chest, heavier and heavier, but I knew she was right. I had known for a very long time, but I had been too willingly led around by the nose like a lamb to do anything about it, and now we were all reaping the consequences.

Alexi nodded, tears gleaming in his eyes. I swept a golden curl away from his forehead and kissed him on the temple.

"I'll prepare the bedchamber," I said, anticipation

coiling in my stomach like a snake. “Can you two tempt him inside?”

Magdalena chuckled. There was no mirth in her voice. “That part’s always been easy.”

don't know how Alexi and Magdalena enticed you away from your work, but they've always been very good at commanding your attention. It was a foolish thing, to make love while the townspeople shook their weapons outside our gates, but arrogance and lust made you reckless. I do not think you truly believed harm would come to any of us. You were too convinced of your own imperviousness. I wonder how many mob uprisings you had seen in your day, how many times you had crushed the peasantry underfoot when they dared take issue with your wanton killing.

I waited for you in white, ever your willing bride. It was an old nightgown in the Victorian style, with pale pink ribbon threaded through the cuffs and a high lace collar. The material skimmed the curves of my body and was nearly transparent in the low light of the wall sconces. I draped myself across the bed, my hair undone and falling to my waist in a waterfall of red.

You had Magdalena pressed against you when you

opened the door and Alexi nipping at your ear, but you stopped short when you saw me. The breath caught in your chest and your pupils went wide with desire. Even after hundreds of years and countless other lovers, I could still arrest you, in the right lighting and with the right pliant expression on my face.

"My wife," you said, taking my face between your hands and tipping my chin up just so into the angle that you so enjoyed. You liked me best when I was like an oil painting, perfectly arranged and silent.

"Yours," I repeated dutifully, my breath hot on your lips. I wondered if you could feel how fast my heart was beating under my skin, smell the fear coming off me like an animal scenting the hunt. I had never felt so terrified in my life, or so exhilarated.

It took me too long to come to my senses and fight back, but now that I was caught in this moment with you, I intended to make up for lost time.

We pulled you onto the bed, Magdalena mewling prettily while Alexi suckled on your little finger. I kissed you and kissed you, driving you back against the pillows with a force that surprised even me. I kissed you the way you had bitten me all those years ago: mercilessly, until you were panting. I pinned you between my thighs and kissed you like I was trying to get back at you for something, like I would never kiss you again. I fit all the love and hate my soul had endured for so many years into that kiss.

Then I flicked my eyes to Magdalena and Alexi, giving

them a signal while you were still murmuring delirious nothings beneath me.

They pinned you down by your shoulders, one on each side. You laughed at first, thinking it a game, but then the smile fell from your face. You tried to wrench out of their grip, but Alexi and Magdalena held you down with the full weight of their bodies, already breaking out in a sweat.

There was only one of you and two of them, but you were older and stronger by far. We didn't have much time.

I reached underneath the bed where I had hidden my contraband and produced an item that felt heavy as treachery in my hands. A rotting rod from a stairwell banister, wrenched free and filed into a sharp point at one end. It was heavy enough to bludgeon a man to death with. Or run him through.

You blanched when you saw it. Genuine terror passed over your face in a wave. Then the anger rose up, and you bared your teeth at me.

"I told you to stay out of my rooms! What stupid little idea has gotten into your head this time? If I die, you all die with me."

It was the gambit of a doomed man.

The first stirrings of power thrummed in my chest. So this was what it felt like, to hold a lover's life in your hand.

"No, we won't," I said. "I read about that too."

This melted the edge off some of your rage, and I saw a flicker of vulnerability cross your face.

"Constanta," you pled, with that same wild raggedness in your voice that rose up when you undressed me, that same desperate sheen in your black eyes I only saw when you called me *treasure*. "I love you. Look at me, Constanta, my jewel, my *wife*. I love you. Don't do this."

I saw every soft moment we had shared flicker over your face, and you were so beautiful. Desperate, vulnerable. Fear for your life made you look like a man who could really love and be loved, like you might hand over your heart and all its secrets without my having to crack your ribs open to get to them. Magdalena must have seen it too; she squeezed her eyes shut and wrenched her face away even as she perspired with the effort of restraining you. Alexi only looked scared, a child caught between two warring parents. I was grateful for his innocence, and his strong arms.

"Constanta," you said again, inclining your mouth up to me as though you were offering a kiss. "Put that down, beloved. I'll forgive you. Stop this now and I'll forgive you, and we'll never speak of it again."

Every kindness you had ever shown me revolted inside me, rioting up in a mutiny against my purpose. Every smile or small gesture was as sharp as a pinprick, inviting me to see the bright spots embroidered through the ugly tapestry of our marriage.

But a few flourishes and embellishments couldn't change the fact that the very fabric of our life together was dark and tangled and suffocating. I had given you a thousand second chances, made a thousand concessions. And this wasn't just about me anymore. It was about Magdalena, and Alexi. How long before you tired of your wind-up soldier and your painted doll and smashed them to pieces?

"Is that what you told the others?" I asked hoarsely. Tears, hot as fresh blood, spilled from my eyes. "Before you killed them?"

Your affect swung from light to dark, a tempestuous shadow settling over your face. Your eyes went from deep, inviting waters to sharpened slate, your mouth tightening into a poison snarl. This was the man I had lived most of my life with: arrogant, cruel, and enraged at the slightest whiff of insurrection.

"Put the stake down, Constanta," you ordered. Harsh, curt. The way you would speak to a dog. "Listen to me. Don't make me angry."

I choked back a sob as I raised the stake above your chest, gripping the wood so hard splinters bit into my bloodless fingers.

I took one ragged breath, two, then squeezed my eyes shut tight.

on't ask me why I did it.

I was tired of being your Mary Magdalene. I was tired of waiting expectantly at your tomb every night for you to rise and bring light into my world once again. I was tired of groveling on my knees and washing blood off your heels with my hair and tears. I was tired of having the air sucked out of my lungs every time your eyes cut right to the heart of me. I was tired of the circumference of the whole universe living in your circled arms, of the spark of life hiding in your kiss, of the power of death lying in wait in your teeth. I was tired of carrying around the weight of a love like worship, of the sickly-warm rush of idolatry coloring my whole world.

I was tired of faithfulness.

I made you into my private Christ, supplicated with my own dark devotions. Nothing existed beyond the range of your exacting gaze, not even me. I was simply a non-entity when you weren't looking at me, an empty vessel waiting to be filled by the sweet water of your attention.

A woman can't live like that, my lord. No one can. Don't ask me why I did it.

God, forgive me.

Christ, forgive me.

I brought the stake down as hard as I could manage. It tore through your flesh, ripping open a cavity in your chest.

You roared in anguish and rage, and Magdalena screamed and screamed, but she didn't let you go. Her steel-sided nature didn't fail her, even as your blood started to seep into her nightdress. Alexi was too shocked to speak, his mouth hanging open with choked, horrified noises coming out of it. But his resolve didn't fail him either.

Letting out a wrenching sob, I pressed down with my whole weight. The stake found its mark, piercing your heart like one of the sorrows of Mary and shattering a rib or two in the process.

It was dirty, difficult work, killing you. You writhed and thrashed, pushing all three of us to the outer limits of our strength. I had to squeeze my knees into your sides and press the stake down with both trembling hands.

Eventually, you let out a horrible, bubbling croak and lay still. Blood bled into our sheets, filling the room with its undeniable fragrance. The sweet, metallic tang filled my nose even as hot tears filled my eyes and spilled over like twin rivers. I had thought you would be as beautiful in death as you were in life, but your face was frozen into a rictus of pain and hatred. Looking on you left me feeling cold, like I was looking at a stranger.

"Is everyone all right?" I managed to ask, my voice barely more than a whisper.

Alexi brought shaky red fingers up to his mouth and lapped at the blood, so dark and sweet. I had never tasted anyone like you, with blood so perfectly aged. It was the rarest, finest vintage in the world, and it held such untapped power. My mouth watered, my gums burning with want.

Magdalena was trembling and sweating like a morphine addict, looking half on the edge of frenzy and half on the edge of unconsciousness.

I was the oldest. I had the most self-control. I could get them out of the room before the bloodlust compelled them to desecrate and drain your body.

I seized Magdalena's wrist and held her fast, tethering our racing heartbeats together as though we were one soul. As though we all had just become forever bonded by our unspeakable act.

"Constance," Alexi said hoarsely. His pupils were blown. "What should we . . .?"

"Drink," I heard myself say. As though from very far away, like I was floating above my own body. "Drink, my loves."

Alexi pressed his mouth to the wound in your chest

and Magdalena tore through your wrist with her teeth, shuddering as your blood burst into her mouth. I bent down and gave you one final kiss, then tipped your head back and nuzzled the cold column of your throat. My stomach was trembling, my fingers clenched and white in the sheets.

I sank my teeth into your neck with a ferocity that surprised me, drinking you down in great, greedy mouthfuls. The taste of you was unparalleled, dark and rich with grace notes of every person you had ever fed from. I clamped a hand around your jaw and bit down harder. My head spun like I had just finished a bottle of whiskey, but still I drank from you, devouring your essence. The power in your veins flooded my system, rushing all the way to the tips of my fingers and toes. The roar of my own heartbeat, the creak of the old house, and the shouts of the rabble outside were suddenly almost painfully loud. The strength of all those years was mine for the taking, and so I took it.

apologize if you were expecting contrition, my lord. I don't have any to muster.

Yes, I knew. I knew what came of drinking the blood of one's sire. I had read about how you killed your maker to seize his power. And I found that I wasn't above it.

I could have turned them away and afforded you some final dignity, but I wanted to hold your power in my mouth, as carefully as a mother cat holds her young, and then swallow until there was nothing of you left.

e fed on you greedily, lapping up every drop. By the time the deed was done, blood was smeared across our faces and down our fronts. Alexi shook, less from fear than from an abundance of energy, and Magdalena's eyes shined like black diamonds, full of life and vigor.

"Jesus," Alexi said, looking down at his stained hands and then over to your body. Blood soaked the sheets and dripped down onto the aged hardwood floor.

It was a bloodbath.

As the bloodlust abated, I slowly returned to myself and took stock of the situation. There was a body to contend with, and a defiled marital bed that would probably never be clean again. And, more pressingly, there were the shouts of the mobs from outside, growing closer and more agitated with every moment. They were at the gates now, hoisting their torches as they rattled the locks. There would be no appeasing them. Certainly not now, with evidence of our crimes laid out in a gruesome tableau.

"Constanta," Magdalena breathed, wiping your blood

from her mouth with the hem of her dress. "What are we going to do?"

They both looked at me with wide eyes, the same eyes they turned on you whenever they didn't know how to handle a situation. You had always been the firm gloved hand on the back of their necks, steering them through life. And now, that responsibility fell to me.

I wiped my brow and took a deep breath. My mind was running quick as a foxhound on the hunt, and a plan was forming.

I sprang up on the bed, bracing my feet on either side of you as I bent down to wrench the stake from your body. It shouldn't have been easy for me: the wood was melded to the cavity of your chest with drying blood and viscera, and the sharpened tip had gone all the way through the mattress. But to my surprise, the stake came away easily in my hands. All at once, I was stronger than I had been before. We all were, I suspected, but I was still the oldest. As far as I knew, I might have been the oldest vampire in all of Europe, now that you were really and truly dead.

The weight of this knowledge pressed down on me like an iron yoke.

"Magdalena, help me move him," I breathed. "Alexi, get the key and go guard the door. I want you to open it, but not until I say so."

Alexi nodded frantically, scrambling off the bed and fumbling the key out of your pocket. I grabbed him by the wrist and pulled him back to me for a quick kiss before I shooed him out of the room. Then I pulled Magdalena into a tight embrace, burying my face into her matted hair.

"What are you going to do?" she asked in a whisper.

I took her face in my hands and kissed her too, tasting the ghost of your blood on her lips.

"I'm going to end this," I said.

ou weighed no more than a child when I hoisted you into my arms. It shouldn't have been possible. You were taller than I was, and I had never had much strength. But I was able to cradle you against my chest and carry you through the doorway and out to the hall, your head lolling against my shoulder.

I took the stairs carefully, Magdalena rushing ahead of me just in case I tripped and fell. Alexi was waiting by the door as requested, every muscle in his body taut with terror.

With you gone, we all felt exposed, vulnerable despite our newfound strength.

"They've broken through the gate," he said, voice tight.

I nodded to Alexi as soon as my bare feet hit the cold floor of the main entryway.

"Let them come," I said. "Unlock the door and then get behind me with your sister. Be ready to run."

Alexi did as he was told, then rushed into the reassuring darkness of the house and Magdalena's open arms. I took a deep breath and shifted your weight in my arms, clutching you tight, and then pushed open the front door.

Twenty men and a handful of enraged mothers come to seek justice for their children stood in the yard, guns brandished and crowbars in their hands, hungry for violence. Their shouts assailed my ears as I stepped into the moonlight, cradling you like a groom might cradle their bride.

The mass stood stock-still when they saw me, the horror on their features illuminated by their flickering torches and lanterns. I suppose I must have looked terrifying; a slip of a girl covered with blood and holding the desiccated body of the monster they had all come to fear. The cries of rage died on their lips as I took a few deliberate steps towards them, feeling the night air on my skin for the first time in ages. Despite the fear pounding in my chest, I felt alive. I felt truly free, no matter what was to become of me.

I knelt and placed your body onto the ground, and in doing so released our hundreds of years together. Grief seized my heart in a vise; it was lined with a sort of euphoria as well. It was as though I had been holding back tears for eons, and now, as I gasped out a sob, something that had been locked up tight inside me was breaking free.

"Here's your demon," I said, my voice fracturing around the tears. "Do with him what you will."

The townspeople descended on your body with a collective shout and I stumbled backwards, sagging against the doorframe of the great old house. They dug their heels into your body and looped a rope around your neck. I dashed back into the house just in time to see one of them raise a scythe high, poised to rend your head from your body.

I slammed the door behind me as it came down with a sickening *shink*.

"Run!" I called to Magdalena and Alexi. I grabbed each of their hands, hauling them up the stairs back to our rooms. "Grab whatever valuables you can carry and run! Once they're done with him, they'll be coming for us."

Magdalena and I stuffed the pockets of our dresses with jewels and golden cigarette cases, and Alexi rifled through your rooms for all the money he could find. Then, without even a chance to change our clothes, we snatched up our coats and shoes and fled out the servants' entrance.

The night was cool and wet, and dew clung to our legs as we raced through the tall grass behind the house. Magdalena stumbled, and Alexi and I hoisted her up, urging her forward. I didn't know where we were going, but I knew we had the whole world ahead of us and certain death behind us. There was nowhere to go but forward.

I looked back only once, just in time to see the villagers hold their torches to our home and cheer as it caught fire. The entire house was up in flame in moments, scorching the small empire you had built. Everything, our clothes, our letters, and the memory of the long days we had spent confined in the country house were consumed by the flames.

"Gone," Alexi babbled, the fire flickering in his wide eyes. "It's all gone."

"We will rebuild," I said, urging him forward. "We will survive. It's what we're best at."

We pulled each other through the muck and the mire, heading for the nearest road.

We held each other and we wept, but we never looked back again, my love. Not once.

ometimes, when I walk through the city, I get a crawling feeling on the back of my neck that compels me to turn around. Sometimes, I think I see your face in the crowd, only for an instant, before you're swept away by the masses again.

e hurried through the wharf, noise and bustle swirling around us as we looked for Alexi's ship. Magdalena was resplendent in a green dress that skimmed her knees, and Alexi looked plucky and seaworthy in suspenders and a newsboy cap. Seagulls swooped and screamed overhead as we three walked arm in arm, craning our necks to read the names of the great ships.

"There it is!" Alexi cried, and we hurried forward to marvel at the ocean liner. It was taller than the apartment building in Paris, strung with cheery flags and thronged by scores of people making their way up the gangplank.

"Do you have your ticket?" Magdalena fretted, straightening Alexi's collar.

"Right here," he said, patting his breast pocket.

"And you promise you'll be safe?" I asked.

Alexi rolled his eyes at me, which earned him a smile. There was my petulant Alexi, as cocksure as ever.

"I'm more dangerous than anyone on that ship," he muttered. "But yes. I promise."

Magdalena and I both covered his face in kisses, not worrying who saw us. We adored him, our golden prince, and even though it broke my heart to let him go, I knew we would all be reunited again soon. I wanted him to be free and happy more than I wanted him shackled at my side.

After much deliberation, handwringing, and tears, we had come to wish each other well before going our separate ways. We had spent so much of our lives together under your shadow, clinging to your apron strings, and it was well past time for us to strike out in the world on our own. Magdalena had enrolled in university in Rome to study politics, and Alexi had booked passage on a ship to America. New York was to be his new playground.

"Promise us that you'll write," Magdalena went on, reddening his cheeks with her lipstick. "Once a week at first, at least! No matter how busy I get with my studies I'll always reply."

"I promise, Maggie," he said, scrunching his nose up at her fretting. But there was a smile lurking beneath his perturbed exterior, and I knew he would keep his promises.

I squeezed Alexi's hands between my own, memorizing their weight and shape. In the coming days, I would often lie in the darkness of my room and trace the outline of his hand into my palm, just to keep his memory close.

"I wish you all the happiness in the world. I'm sorry I can't come with you."

"You need to find your own way, I know." He gave

me a mischievous smirk. "We'll be seeing each other sooner than you think, though, when I've got my name in lights and you come see me performing in one of those big American theatres."

We all started as the ship's horn trumpeted, calling the last of the passengers on board. Alexi gave me one more firm kiss, and then he was off, hoisting himself up the gangplank along with the other passengers. I watched him go with tears in my eyes and my heart in my mouth. Moments later he leaned over the railing of the ship, snatching off his hat and waving at us. Magdalena shouted his name and waved goodbye with her handkerchief while I cried.

We stayed there until the ship was so far on the horizon it was barely more than a speck. Then Magdalena pulled me into a tight hug, rubbing her hand in soothing circles on my back.

"He'll be all right," she soothed. "He's a brave boy."

"He'll be better than all right," I said, taking her offered handkerchief and daubing my eyes. "He'll be truly great."

I walked her arm in arm to her carriage, moving at a brisk clip. She had sent her belongings ahead of her to Italy, and had lingered in the city for a few more days to see Alexi off, and to save our last few hours together. We had spent much of that time either in bed or exploring Antwerp together, traipsing down alleyways and slipping in and out of bars and watching the blush of dawn paint the sky. It had been almost a month since we escaped the house in the country, and I was finally able to walk down the street without my stomach tightening at the thought of how angry you would be at me for breaking curfew. Slowly, the noose of your love was loosening around my neck.

I clutched Magdalena's hands when we came to her carriage, my own hands trembling. I had been with all of you for so long that the thought of walking through the world on my own was as terrifying as it was exhilarating.

"You must take care of yourself," I said. "If anything were to happen to you, I would die."

"Sweet Constanta. Come here."

She pulled me into the forgiving dark of her carriage, took my face between her hands, and kissed me. It was a long, deep kiss, gentle and slow, and when we pulled away both our faces were wet with tears.

Magdalena daubed at her eyes with her handkerchief, then wiped my cheeks clean.

"There," she pronounced. "As pretty and brave as any storybook princess. I will miss you so desperately, my love. Have you decided yet where you will go first?"

"Not yet," I murmured. "But I want to travel. I want to see my own Romania in the springtime again. I want to meet absolutely everyone and make a score of friends and spend every night out in the world, surrounded by people. And I think, someday, I would like to fall in love again."

"I want that for you. So fiercely. Be well until we meet again. It will be sooner than either of us think. I know it."

I stepped outside the carriage and stood there with my hand on the door for a long moment, marveling at her beauty one last time. She gave me one of her wry, clever smiles, and blew me a kiss. I could almost feel it burning against my cheek as I stepped away and let the carriage roll on past.

I watched until the carriage had been swept away by traffic, giving one last little wave as it rounded the corner and took my Magdalena off into a new life. Then I took a step into the crowd and let the city swallow me whole.

nd so, my love, we have come to the end of our lives together. Your bones are moldering in a charred grave somewhere in the French countryside and I am moving through the world, truly free for the first time in my long life. My nights are full of long walks and the scent of ocean breezes and the sound of people singing. Sometimes, I hear your voice in my dreams and I wake with a start, but I'm getting better at soothing myself back to sleep these days. Perhaps in time I will stop asking God for His forgiveness. Perhaps I will be able to uncurl the defenses around my heart and let someone see me the way you saw me, vulnerable and naked and totally trusting.

I have one final promise to make to you, one I hope I will never break. I promise to live, richly and shamelessly, and with my arms wide open to the world. If there was any part left of you at the end that wished for our great happiness, that truly wanted what was best for us, I think it would be pleased to hear me say it. I do not know if I have justified my choice to you, but I think I have justified it to myself, and that has brought me peace enough.

So I will put down my pen. I will tuck these pages away in a drawer and tuck the memories of you away in my mind, and I will go out into the world and live. I will build an undying family of my own, and there will be no raised voices or locked doors between us. Your memory will fade to shadow and I shall never speak your name again, not even when I tell my lovers the story of how we two met. There will only be sweetness and kindheartedness, and a hundred years of bliss.

AN ENCORE OF ROSES

he spotlight poured down over me like long-forgotten sunlight as I paced the stage, my voice carrying easily through the theater. The audience was rapt in silence, wrapped around my little finger as I recited my lines. The play was a tragedy in the classical style, all melodrama and fake blood, and my animal nature thrilled at the carnage of it, especially on that night. That night, I wasn't the only predator in the house.

I played my heart out, angling every pithy joke and heartrending line to the stage-right box, where I knew hungry eyes were watching. Two lovely pairs of eyes, chestnut-brown and sable-black. Even under the blazing stage lights, I shivered at the thought of those eyes on me, eating me up from afar.

I used to think nothing could beat the euphoric rush of applause, but as I clasped hands with my castmates and took my bows, something even stronger cut through the roar of clapping and cheering. Anticipation.

It flooded my veins like the finest absinthe. By the time

I staggered off the stage and navigated my way past jostling bodies to the dressing rooms, I was quite drunk on it.

They found me before I found them, because they always do. After tossing my costume on the hanger and peeling the mic tape off my face without so much as bothering to scrub off the greasepaint, I dashed out of the dressing room and nearly collided with them both. Two otherworldly figures, so beautiful it hurt to look at them.

"Constance!" I exclaimed. "Maggie! Oh, you made it!"

I threw myself into Magdalena's arms because she was closest, and she kissed me without hesitation. I reached out a hand for Constanta and she laced her fingers through mine, then covered my face in a flurry of kisses. One of them, I couldn't say which, pressed a fragrant bouquet of crimson roses into my arms.

The first kiss from Magdalena always felt like nicking your finger on the edge of a knife: a sharp shock, and then throbbing warmth. Constanta, on the other hand, was like slipping into a warm bath after a day of hard labor. All relief and unwinding muscles.

"Alexi," Constanta murmured against my mouth, cradling my cheeks in her hands. "Oh, little Alexi, we've missed you so terribly."

We were making a scene right there in the backstage corridor, but I didn't care. Magdalena and Constanta were here. People could walk around us, or look the other way if our display displeased them.

I encircled them both with my arms, pulling them into a tight hug. I was lightheaded with ecstasy, being pressed between them. All was right in the world again.

Constanta was still wearing her hair long, swirled up on top of her head in a messy twist. Tendrils of red fell down around her face and I touched them, delighted by this tiny, imperfect detail. She hadn't aged a moment since I had last seen her, and the creases around her eyes only showed when she smiled intensely, as she was doing now.

"You were a marvel," she said.

"A revelation," Magdalena chimed in, stepping aside to let two other actors pass. They craned their necks to look at her as they did so, and I couldn't blame them. She was wearing back-seam stockings, a tight plum pencil skirt, and a silk blouse that showed off her light brown decolletage.

"It wasn't my best work," I said. "You missed me as Puck a few years ago; I was absolutely incandescent."

"I know," Constanta said in her soothing voice. "But I was in Cyprus with Henri and Sasha . . ."

"And I was advising a Vatican council on the new pope, you know that," Magdalena said, just as kindly but much less apologetically. She loved her work pulling strings behind the seats of international power just as much as she loved us. I long ago accepted that our marriage bed would have to be shared with her scheming.

"I know, I know," I muttered, and I found that I was still hurt they weren't able to make it. It was less about the play, though it was very good, and more about the fact that it had been nearly three decades since we'd all been together. We almost never went that long between visits. I had dropped in on Constanta for a few hours' tryst during a layover on my last European tour, but it wasn't the same. Too much time had passed since we were all reunited.

But they have other lives and other lovers now, I reminded myself as the girls fussed over me and kissed and complimented me. *I'm not the sun in their sky anymore.*

The thought made the bottom drop out of my stomach, but I gave them a smile all the same. If there's one thing I'm good at, it's smiling through pain.

"Come on," I said, tugging them towards the exits. "I'm dying for a coffee and a sweet."

"You're still eating?" Magdalena said, baffled. She didn't add "human food" to the end of that sentence, since we were currently surrounded by mortals.

"I am a hedonist in every sense," I declared, taking their hands in each of my own. "I shall savor all the sensory pleasures of the world until I can no longer bear them."

"You haven't changed at all," Constanta said, so fondly that I thought my heart might burst.

e stalked the rain-slick city streets until we came across my favorite Italian bakery, tucked between a laundromat and a pawn shop down an unassuming alley. I'd traveled the world in the hundred-odd years I'd been alive, but I always seemed to find myself back in New York. I loved the cramped, unexpected charm of the place, the way it distilled down so many different languages and cultures into something heady and distinctly American. America suited me, despite her puritanical mores and gross institutional mismanagement. She was brazen and loud and in love with herself, just like me.

I ordered a café au lait and a cream puff, both easy enough on the stomach that I could enjoy the taste without getting sick. I'd noticed the changes Constanta warned me about in recent years, the pallor coming into my skin, the waning interest in any sustenance other than blood, but I intended to wring every drop of enjoyment out of eating until I lost my taste for it.

"Try it," I said, holding out a dollop of whipped cream on my little finger for Magdalena.

"I'm on a diet," she said drolly.

"It will disappear on your tongue; it's just a tiny bit of cream and sugar. Live a little, Maggie."

Magdalena acquiesced to my request, circling my wrist with her fingers and bringing the whipped cream to her mouth. She closed her lips around my finger, suckling in a way that sent a jolt of electricity down my spine.

"Oh, that is good," she admitted, dark eyes widening. She picked up some cream on her finger and held it out to Constanta, who eyed it warily.

"I'm older than you are," she reminded us, as though we could forget. Constanta may have been one of the oldest vampires currently living, and though she was gracious and gentle with her power, it was evident in the way she carried herself, the way her eyes flashed in the dark. We all became more powerful that night we killed our sire and drank from his veins, but Constanta was the eldest, so she reaped the most potent benefits.

"It won't hurt," Magdalena promised. "Alexi is right."

Constanta opened her mouth for Magdalena and lapped up the sweet treat. Her eyes went wide at the flavor, and she made a pleased little hum in the back of her throat. Magdalena chuckled and kissed her with such a swift, thoughtless tenderness that I ached. They were so perfect together, and they were mine.

At least, I thought they were still mine.

"How are your lovers?" I asked, because it was the polite thing to do. I was also, perhaps, curious.

Constanta's face lit up, and she leaned a little further

over the table. The sleeves of her billowing white blouse rippled elegantly and the golden cross around her neck glinted. She always enjoyed flouting the superstition that religious icons were anathema to us, and I think part of her really still believed in that old story about blood and suffering.

"Henri and Sasha are as sweet as the day I met them. So many small gestures of loving kindness. Henri cleans the blood out of my clothes after every hunt and tucks flowers in the pockets, and Sasha is always bringing home books and highlighting her favorite passages for me to read. We're summering in Romania this year. I want to show them where I was born."

"It was brave of you," Magdalena said, stealing another nibble of cream, "to turn others after what happened to us."

A shadow passed over Constanta's face, but only for a moment.

"The bond we had with him was built on control and deceit. I've always been honest with Henri and Sasha, and they've always been honest with me. We allow each other our freedom."

She didn't need to specify the "him" she was talking about. My throat got a little tighter as unpleasant memories pressed in. We don't speak his name anymore, but he's impossible to forget.

"And what do they think of the undying life?" I asked, curious about these new vampires I've never met who have so captured my dear Constanta's heart. There aren't many people in the café to overhear, and I've never been one for subtlety anyway.

"They've taken to it like fish to water," Constanta said with a chuckle. "Henri is as insatiable as you were when you were young. Do you remember how we had to teach you restraint?"

"He drained so many milkmaids and messenger boys," Magdalena said fondly.

I wrinkled my nose at their teasing.

"I learned fast. You would be proud of me, Constance. I've barely killed anyone for ages. Discretion, isn't that what you always say? Only taking as much as you need so as not to draw suspicion with a trail of bodies?"

"Good for you," Magdalena said, ever one for cleverness. "That will allow you to stay in one place as long as you like with no police or priests banging down your door. At least, until they start to notice that you don't age. I do so hate moving all the time. Italy suits me."

"And how is your Italian thrall?" I asked, sucking down a little of my café au lait. Constanta had always been drawn to building little families wherever she goes, but Magdalena tended to prefer solitary human companions who could offer stimulating conversation and a steady supply of blood.

"Oh, Fabrizio? Wonderful, wonderful. So attentive and devoted. He reads to me from the papers every evening and he's even shifted his sleep schedule so he's awake at my hours."

"You've been together a decade," Constanta noted. "You should let me turn him for you."

"That's kind of you, but I like Fabrizio just the way he is. The undying life isn't for him; he's too in love with life."

"But he'll *age*," I whispered, as though it was a curse.

Magdalena shrugged. "And die, yes. Or maybe we'll part ways sometime in the future. Nothing is certain, little Alexi."

"I'm not so little anymore."

"Yes, but you'll always be the youngest."

Constanta stepped in before Magdalena and I could get into one of our friendly sniping matches.

"What about you, Alexi? Have you taken any lovers since we last spoke? Perhaps found a thrall of your own?"

I suddenly felt very put on the spot, and I swallowed down a little coffee with a gulp. I hadn't taken a lover in a long time, I realized. I drank from strangers, or sometimes my friends if they were feeling adventurous. I brought people into my bed for a night or two, victim or no. But when I thought of a lover, I thought of Magdalena and Constanta. Everyone else paled in comparison to their radiance.

"I, uh . . . Well, no. I haven't had occasion to."

Magdalena's brows creased in thought, and Constanta opened her mouth, probably to say something encouraging, but then the waitress appeared at our table with the check. I smiled broadly at her, banishing my momentary glumness, and flirted with her so much that Magdalena rolled her eyes.

Then we ducked out into the night, three beautiful villains, and joked and laughed among ourselves all the way back to my studio.

y studio was modest, not like the grand apartments and crumbling old estates we had all once lived in together, but it had its own kind of charm. Dripping candles were affixed to the stem of wine bottles, and a deck of gilded cards had been left out on the kitchen table from my last round of drinking and petty gambling with my actor friends. The curtains were red damask, heavy enough to block out the light of the sun, and the threadbare rugs underfoot were vintage and Persian, almost as old as me.

I took Magdalena and Constanta's coats, still a gentleman despite my libertine ways, and hung them up on the coat hook by the door.

We were on each other in an instant.

Constanta slid her arms around my shoulders and melted into my kiss while Magdalena mouthed insistently at my neck. I snaked an arm around her waist and pulled her close, alternating between their two mouths in the dim light of my studio. I lost myself in the rich tide of their love, buoyed along by a hundred tiny touches and soft sounds of pleasure. Happiness beyond comprehension washed over me.

Magdalena was here with me, my stern, beautiful Magdalena with her heart like liquid gold. And so was Constanta, lovely, dreamy Constanta with her mouth shaped like compassion. My sisters, my most intimate friends. My girls, *mine*.

Here is a secret: I may be fond of the games of love, but I am fiercely possessive in my own way. A little bit of my heart travels with them when they circumnavigate the world, and I am always desperate to be reunited with it. We three were made to fit together, and I am not entirely myself unless I am nestled between the two of them.

We are children of the same rotten family, survivors of the same intimate war. We will always be lovers, for ever bonded, across distance and time.

"I missed you," I sighed, my breath stirring the loose curls of Constanta's hair as it ghosted across Magdalena's lips.

"Which one of us?" Magdalena asked with one of her throaty laughs.

"Both of you," I said, my fingers already making short work of the buttons on her blouse. She batted my hand away lightly, a smile on her lips.

"Patience, little Alexi. It's been so long since I've seen you. You must let me enjoy myself."

Constanta gave me one last lingering kiss before stepping into the dark of my small living room.

"I'm going to freshen up," she said in a knowing singsong. "I'll leave you to each other."

I let out a needy whine of protest, but Magdalena was having none of it. She thrilled at the chance to have me to herself, and she wasn't going to waste the opportunity.

Magdalena slid her fingers into my hair and tugged lightly, administering just enough pain to be interesting. I whined again, this time in pleasure.

"My favorite masochist," Magdalena purred, dropping her lips to mine. She held me with a firm grip on my chin, her fingertips leaving divots in my skin. I lost myself in the heady sensation of being claimed by her, possessed by her.

"Surely not your favorite," I said, chasing her kiss when she pulled away. "What would Fabrizio say?"

Magdalena dug her fingernails into my flesh and I gave a hiss of pleasured pain.

"Fabrizio is mine to do with as I wish and right now, so are you," she said. Oh, how I loved this game. The game of hurt and denial that always ended in ecstasy. Magdalena was the finest player I had ever met on the board, and this was her opening gambit.

I responded in kind, nipping at her fingers with my sharp eye teeth. Magdalena swatted my cheek, briskly enough to sting pleasantly but not hard enough to do any damage. It was worlds away from the times I have been hit in anger, and all the sweeter for the delicate restraint with which Magdalena flicked her wrist.

Magdalena didn't quite move fast enough to spare her

pretty fingers from my bite, however, and a ruby bead appeared on her index finger.

"Suck it off for me, Alexi," she requested in that imperious voice.

"Such a princess," I scoffed, but I was happy to oblige.

I opened my mouth and slid the wet pad of my tongue along her finger, savoring the little shiver that went through her body. Queenly Magdalena did her best to hide it, but I knew the effect I had on her. We had always been weak for each other, falling into bed together with all the shameless urgency of teenagers.

I suckled off the droplet of blood, moaning low in my throat at the taste. No one tasted like my Magdalena, as rich and sweetly spiced. No one could compare with the delicious patina of time that swirled through her veins, except perhaps Constanta.

"Playing your games?" Constanta murmured, appearing from the bathroom. She had discarded her trousers and stood bare-legged in that billowing white shirt, her red hair falling loose around her face. It almost drove me to my knees, how perfect she looked. Constanta was beautiful enough to make an apostle out of an apostate, and I was no exception. I wanted to worship at the cathedral of her body until she cried out like ringing Sunday mass bells.

"Always," Magdalena said, withdrawing her finger from my mouth with a pop. "He's so needy, Constanta."

"Then nothing has changed," Constanta said with a chuckle that shot through me like electricity. I would have crawled to her if she asked me, on my hands and knees like a dog.

"Constance," I said, my voice hoarse with desire. "Please."

"Use your words, Alexi," Magdalena said, threading her long-nailed fingers through my curls. "Ask for what you want."

"I want both of you. At the same time. Please."

Constanta just smiled that Mona Lisa smile as she sank down on the edge of my bed, opening her arms to me. I tugged Magdalena along with me as I kicked off my shoes and shucked off my jacket, surrendering myself to Constanta's expert ministrations.

She pressed me back against the bed with her kisses while Magdalena made short work of my belt.

"Eager," Magdalena said with a toothy grin, squeezing me through my jeans. I tried to come up with a pithy reply, but the pressure of her agile fingers stole my breath. She wasn't lying; I was hard already and straining against the denim. It had been a tiny eternity since I had last seen my girls, and I was eager to make up for lost time.

"True," Constanta mused, her brown eyes roving over my face. "But sullen."

"I'm not sullen," I shot back, slipping my hands under her blouse and spreading my fingers across her bare back. Her brows knit together in that sympathetic, knowing way that always cut to the quick of me. Damn her knowing instincts.

"Yes, you were, in the café. There's a shadow behind your eyes, sweet prince. What's wrong?"

I swallowed hard, partially because Constanta was finding me out and partially because Magdalena had lowered her head to mouth me through my jeans.

"Nothing's wrong," I huffed. "I've just missed you is all."

"Mmm," Constanta hummed, not convinced. But she still kissed me, and that was all that mattered. I just wanted to be close to her and Magdalena, as close as skin on skin and blood mingling with blood. Surely, that would put all my treacherous thoughts to rest. That would make me feel whole again.

Magdalena crawled up the bed towards me, as lithe and dangerous as a cat on the prowl, and wrapped her slim fingers around my neck. She barely applied any pressure, but it was enough to make my throat flutter with anticipation. My eyes slid shut of their own accord as Constanta freed me from the cage of my jeans. My hips bucked beneath her, already moving of their own accord.

This. I had missed this.

"Please, Maggie," I begged. "Just a little harder."

Magdalena obliged as Constanta took me into her mouth expertly, nearly driving me to the brink of madness.

"God," I rasped, pressing up against Magdalena's grasp. Oh, she was wicked. She knew how to squeeze the breath from me without cutting off circulation or suffocating me entirely. She could hold me like that for as long as she wanted, and I would be powerless against her. "Jesus Christ, Maggie."

"Blasphemy," Constanta chided with a smile, then laved me with her tongue. I gasped despite myself, curling my fingers into the sheets.

"I missed you," I rasped. "I missed you both so much."

"Is that why you've been in such a dark mood all evening?" Constanta asked, circling my tip with her tongue like it was hard candy.

"*Constanta*," I groaned. "Is this really the time?"

"It's the perfect time," Magdalena said, and drove me into the mattress with a force that would have bruised a human lover. They were in on this together, I could tell from the sparkling glances they shared as they tormented me. I wanted to call them off, to gather myself up and pull myself off the bed. But I loved this too much. I loved being unmade by them.

"Tell me what's wrong," Constanta said, playing with me idly with her fingers. She squeezed and ran a thumb along the length of me, as though I was her favorite toy. "And then we can continue."

"Blackmail," I accused.

"You love it."

"Touché."

Magdalena kissed me so soundly I almost forgot my name, her grip on my throat secure and unwavering. Then she nipped me with those sharp teeth, drawing blood from my lower lip. Her hot, searching tongue lapped it up. When she spoke, her voice was rough with bloodlust.

"Answer her, Alexi. So I can have you properly."

I writhed under their expert torments, equal parts

blissful and debased. I shouldn't say anything. I should keep it all to myself, locked up tight in a corner of my mind that I never examined, and then everything would be all right. What if I shared my feelings and they grew cold against me, or left me alone in New York? What if they took offense at my words, or exploded in rage like lovers from the past?

Constanta squeezed so mercilessly that I had no choice but to let out a helpless gasp, and then the words came tumbling out of me.

"You don't care for me the same way anymore," I blurted.

Instantly, the room went quiet. Magdalena released my throat and Constanta tucked me back into my jeans, her face stricken as though she had just been caught in some indiscretion. For one horrible instant, I thought I had shattered our love to pieces. I pressed up onto my elbows, breathing hard, tears prickling at the back of my eyes.

But then Constanta reached out and stroked my cheek. Constanta, my guardian angel. My protector.

"Is that what you really think?" she asked quietly.

I looked from her to Magdalena. Magdalena's eyes were dark, as though she were riddling out some international conflict. That same line was between her brows, like she wanted to fix me with her diplomacy and nepotism.

"I'm just worried is all," I muttered, feeling suddenly embarrassed.

I shouldn't have said anything. I should have kept my fool mouth shut.

Magdalena and Constanta exchanged a glance, and then they both embraced me with a ferocity that took my breath away. I held on to them tightly, letting them rock me like a fussy child.

"Alexi, Alexi," Constanta murmured. "I couldn't stop loving you if my life depended on it. Even if you were sunlight itself, I would still scorch myself to be close to you."

"And I would raze a city to the ground if it meant making you smile," Magdalena swore.

"What brought this on?" Constanta asked.

I shrugged, and found to my horror that there was a tightness in my throat. I would *not* cry.

"It's just been so long since I've seen either of you. And you have other lovers now, other lives."

"You're my whole world, Alexi," Constanta said, cutting me off. Her eyes flashed in the dark, a reminder of her preternatural power. It made me shudder, that power, but it never made me feel unsafe. If anything, the knowledge of what Constanta could do made me feel cared for, like a treasured jewel in a fairy tale guarded by the strongest spell.

"Is this about Fabrizio?" Magdalena asked, nestling closer to me on the bed. She laid her head on my shoulder. "It isn't the same, Alexi. We love each other, in our way, but I could never love him the way I love you. You're my family. My past and my future."

"Henri and Sasha have become family to me," Constanta chimed in, raising my hand to her mouth and kissing the tips of my five fingers. "But they will never be you, Alexi. It isn't a contest, there are no winners or losers. There is only love. And I'm happy to tell you that as many times as you need to hear it, from now until the end of the Earth."

"Thank you," I said quietly, and oh, now the tears were coming. I buried my face in Constanta's shirt, hoping the dark would hide them, and scrubbed at my cheeks with the back of my hand.

"Poor prince," Magdalena cooed. "We've left you alone for too long."

"We must remedy that immediately," Constanta said, drawing me to her breast. She hugged me tightly, then kissed me on the mouth so sweetly it almost ignited a fresh round of tears. "I was only going to stay a week, but would you mind terribly if—"

"Please stay," I said, gripping her tighter. I promised myself I would never beg for anything from anyone. I had been subjugated in one relationship and never wanted to be in another, but Constanta didn't make me feel small or weak. She made me feel strong and whole, like I had a right to ask for what I wanted. So I did. "Just a little while longer. I've missed you both so badly."

"You never said so, silly boy," Magdalena said, pulling me into her arms next. She rubbed soothing circles onto my back with her hands. "Whenever I call I hear nothing but glowing stories of your friendships and your time on the stage. All it would have taken from you was one word and I would have dropped everything and come running."

"I didn't want to interrupt your business," I sniffed.

"My business can wait. You, my love, are the premiere among my concerns."

She kissed me deeply, and my anxiety began to melt away little by little. How could I be worried when Constanta and Magdalena were in my arms, real and solid as the first time we had met? It seemed foolish suddenly to have ever been afraid that they would be cross with me. They were my girls, after all. We understood each other intimately, better than any other human or vampire ever could. We were bonded eternally.

"Please," I said into Magdalena's mouth. "Please can I have you?"

"Yes, my love," she said. Somewhere along the way, she had already discarded her stockings, and she shuddered in pleasure as I pushed her skirt up around her waist. I thrilled at the flash of her thighs, at the black silk peeking out between her legs. But more than that, I thrilled at the sound of her voice. "Anytime you want me, I'm yours."

"Constanta?" I asked, reaching a hand out to her and pulling her close. I kissed the pale column of her throat, entranced by her taste, her scent. "Will you have me?"

"Now, and always," Constanta said, slipping off her shirt and dropping it onto the floor. "I want you to take your pleasure from me. Be greedy, my darling. Be jealous, if you want. I will always be here for you, whenever you call."

I ran my tongue along the curve of her jaw, then dropped my mouth to grinning Magdalena's lips.

"You both unmake me," I said hoarsely.

"We'll stay as long as you want us to," Magdalena said, and let loose a soft little gasp as I discarded her skirt and started to unfasten the buttons of her blouse. "And then when we cross the ocean again we'll take you with us. We'll find you a new theatre, a new rapt audience. We need never be parted again."

"I'll hold you to that," I replied, discarding my shirt and my jeans in an unceremonious heap on the floor.

I let Constanta run her hands along my bare chest, then dug my nails into Magdalena's hips as I entered her. She raked her nails down my back, hard enough to leave marks. *Good*, I thought, through the diaphanous haze of lust as Magdalena bucked against me and Constanta lay down beside me. *Let us mark each other.*

"Alexi, Alexi," Constanta sighed with her arms and legs open.

"Constance," I breathed as I pleasured her with my fingers. I held Magdalena tighter, drawing her close as our bodies intertwined. The air in the room was warm and close, wrapping us in a heady fog. All I could hear was my own breathing and Magdalena's little whimpers and Constanta's happy sighing. "Maggie."

We worshipped each other until dawn, losing ourselves in our love for each other. When dawn came, I slumbered in both their arms, secure in the knowledge that I would never have to be alone again.

Acknowledgments

This book was passed through so many talented, loving hands on its way to completion, and I am immensely grateful to everyone who lent me their time, encouragement, and expertise in the writing process. Thank you to all my wonderful critique partners and beta readers who helped make this book into what it is today. Thank you to my fantastic agent Tara for encouraging me and advocating for me, and my great love Kit for supporting me and being my sounding board. Thank you to Celine, my first editor, who helped me weave a coherent book from the first inklings of a story all the way through to final edits. Thank you to the whole team at Orbit US and UK, especially Nadia, Anna, Angeline, Tim, Joanna, and everyone else who helped bring this book to an even wider audience. And, of course, thank you to the readers who have championed this project at every stage with so much enthusiasm. Your support means the world to me.